TIME UNDERGROUND
American Epochs: Volume II

By Todd McClimans

OVERDUE
BOOKS

An Imprint of Northampton House Press

TIME UNDERGROUND. Copyright 2015 by Todd McClimans. All rights reserved, including the right to reproduce this book, or portions thereof, in any form.

Cover design by Tim Ogline, incorporating art by Naia Poyer.

First Northampton House Press edition, 2015. ISBN 978-1-937997-62-5.

Library of Congress Control Number: 2015933924.

www.northampton-house.com.

Overdue Books and Northampton House Press are pending trademarks of Northampton House LLC.

10 9 8 7 6 5 4 3 2

TIME UNDERGROUND

Oh I heard Queen Victoria say,
That if we would forsake,
Our native land of slavery,
And come across de lake;
Dat she was standing on de shore,
Wid arms extended wide,
To give us all a peaceful home,
Beyond de rolling tide;
Farewell, ole Master, don't think hard of me,
I'm traveling on to Canada, where all de slaves are free.

- Sarah Bradford, *Harriet Tubman, the Moses of Her People*

1858

Two boys stole through the quiet Maryland backcountry under a thin shard of half-moon. They'd sloshed through icy creeks and inlets on bare, blistered feet, slunk from tree to tree through thickets between sleeping plantations, and had crossed miles of frozen furrows and empty fields.

They finally stopped to lean against two large pines, puffing great clouds of frozen breath, slumped in exhaustion.

"How—how much farther, Jonah?" one asked the other between gasps. He was thin and slight, an undersized scarecrow with midnight skin, shivering in a threadbare cotton shirt big enough for someone twice his size.

"Gotta go all night, Britt," his companion answered. "Find a place to hole-up 'fore dawn." Jonah touched his brother's shoulder. He was the oldest, fifteen, lean, but well-muscled.

Britt bent over, hands propped on knees. "I—I can't—"

The baying of bloodhounds, like alarm bells in the distance, cut his words off.

"Run!" Jonah shoved him forward.

They tore across the field, looking back over their shoulders.

Just before the tree line at the end of the field, Britt tripped, gave a yelp and went down in a heap.

"Get up!" Jonah yelled.

But his brother only groaned, writhing and clutching at an already swelling foot.

"Come on! You gotta get up!" Jonah pressed. "They comin'!" He yanked the boy up by one skinny arm.

Britt tried to take a step, but his face contorted and he crumpled into Jonah's arms. Tears streamed from his wide eyes. "I just can't!"

More howls and barking cut the air, closer now. A flurry of lanterns spilled into the field, the cries of men punctuated by the boom of a shotgun.

Jonah swore. "Get on my back!"

"You ain't gonna carry me all the way to Canaan."

"The heck I ain't!" Jonah hoisted the boy onto his back, then stumbled on through briars and bushes and into the dark stand of trees. Brambles tore at his face and arms. Dry branches snapped like gunshots as he pushed through more thickets. After a hundred yards, an exposed root grabbed his foot, and they went down in a heap together.

Britt rolled off his brother's back and lay face-up on the pine-needle covered path. Tears cut lines through the grime on his cheeks. "You gotta leave me, Jonah!"

The lanterns were now halfway across the field. Black silhouettes of hunting hounds strained against taut chains. Jonah swore again. "Get up this tree. I'll draw 'em away from you."

He hefted Britt by the waist until the boy could grasp the lowest branch and pull himself up.

"Stay hid," Jonah ordered. "I'll come back for you soon."

Britt climbed higher, then higher still, and into the shadow of the trunk. "Don' let 'em get you, Jonah."

The hounds and hunters reached the woods. Jonah whooped and took off at a dead run. The frantic baying of the bloodhounds grew louder still, the dogs hallooing in chorus, as if certain any moment they'd close their jaws on a fleeing ankle or catch the rugged hem of a runaway's trousers.

But the hounds went no farther. Jonah stopped, looked back. Circles of light now surrounded the tree in which his brother was hidden. Two shotgun blasts rang out.

"No," Jonah whispered. He took a step back toward the ring of jeering men, then stopped. Tears burned his eyes. He lowered his head.

"I'm sorry, Britt. I'm sorry."

He turned away, stepped deeper into the shadow of the trees, and disappeared.

ONE:
THE PRESENT

Kristi Connors sat scowling on a seat near the back of a crowded train car, hands clenched around a magazine rolled as tight as a baton. The issue of *Soccer World* had an article about a national tournament, a tournament *her* travel team would be playing in that weekend. And where was she? Not in a hotel with her teammates, making midnight crank calls to the front desk, drinking Mountain Dew for breakfast. Not scoring goals and winning medals.

No, of course not. Instead, she was on a train headed to the middle of nowhere to do the Chicken Dance in an ugly powder-blue dress.

Intermittent snores like a snuffling pig escaped the open mouth of the old woman asleep in the seat next to her. The reek of the woman's cheap drugstore perfume burned Kristi's nose. On the woman's lap sat a huge pink, plastic purse. The head of a bug-eyed Chihuahua no bigger than a sewer rat stuck out of the top. A little pink bow was fixed between the dog's bat-ears.

Kristi shifted in her seat and the little rat growled, baring tiny, pointed teeth.

"Shut up," she hissed and stuffed her hands under her legs, pressing closer to the wall so she only took up half her seat. She gave the dog a dirty look, then leaned her head against the sun-warmed window glass and gazed out. Nothing but endless fields, brown blurs whizzing past.

When the train entered a tunnel, the reflection of a slender girl, three months shy of her thirteenth birthday, stared back. A pretty girl, despite the scowl and the three pimples dotting the chin and cheeks of her smooth, chocolate-hued skin. Her thick black hair was braided into tight zigzags and a ponytail threaded with red beads rattled and bounced against the back of her neck.

She narrowed her eyes, and frowned, practicing the look she'd give her father when he picked her up at the train station. She stuck her tongue out at the reflection.

The train left the dark tunnel and passed back into daylight, whizzing by a large green farmhouse. A lump formed in Kristi's throat. Farms made her think of Ty.

She sighed and ran her hands over her braids. The stupid little rat-dog yipped as if she'd pinched it. Kristi jumped and stuffed her hands back under her legs and heaved a sigh.

The old woman gave a gargled snort. She smacked her lips a few times, then opened her eyes and reached a wrinkled hand to stroke the dog's taut neck. "There, there, Precious. Leave the nice girl alone."

Precious? Really?

Kristi faked a smile for the old woman and turned away again.

It wasn't *fair*! Nobody'd ever asked what *she* thought about her dad getting remarried. He didn't care that she hated gap-toothed Maria. That she silently wished poisonous mutant slugs would slither into the woman's pretty little ears while she was sleeping, and slowly, painfully, eat away her brain, if she even had one. He didn't care that she hated gap-toothed Maria and her know-it-all daughter, Brittany, who never stopped talking about clothes and shoes and – *ugh!*

Kristi gritted her teeth and leaned back, wishing she could talk to Ty right now. He could've helped her come up with a scheme to get out of going to the wedding. But that wasn't going to happen. She'd never get to talk to him again.

It made her head hurt and chest ache to think Ty had been dead for over 150 years. Thomas, too.

But pride in her friends, and what they'd accomplished, soon overtook the ache. When she'd left Ty and Thomas behind on that colonial farm back in 1780, they'd just been a couple of out-of-place English kids with no family and no country—no *time*—of their own. Since she'd returned to her own place and time, she'd looked up Ty and Thomas Jordan on Wikipedia at least a hundred times. They'd gone on to Pennsylvania's first medical school and then made a fortune as farmers and surgeons. Later in their lives they'd served as conductors on the Underground Railroad, worked with Harriet Tubman, and even met with Abraham Lincoln about the Emancipation Proclamation. The two of them had done so much good in the world. Things that really mattered.

Yet here she was, still stuck being treated like a little girl who wasn't even allowed to choose whether or not she had to go to a stupid wedding, or stay at a stupid boarding school. As if she was too *young* to make her own decisions. She snorted. If her dad only knew what she'd been through on her own trip back to the past— the battles, tending the wounded soldiers, facing that alternate future. Then he wouldn't *dare* to treat her like a child anymore.

But she'd never spoken to her father, or anyone else, about her adventures traveling through time. How could she? Who would even believe her?

She clenched her eyes shut and thought hard about her experiences in 1780. The memories did feel a little hazy. A chill ran up her spine. What if it really had been just a delusional nightmare? What if she really hadn't known Ty Jordan? Could a person really go back in time to thwart a conspiracy to destroy the American Revolution? The more she thought about it, the more far-fetched it all seemed. The more it seemed as though she maybe belonged in a nut house.

Cold drops of sweat beaded on her forehead. Her chest tightened until she couldn't pull in a full breath. She leaned forward, ignoring the suspicious growls of the rat-dog, and dug into her backpack. There, buried at the bottom, wrapped in a towel, she felt the time machine, a cold metal rod the length of two paper towel rolls. She let out a long, relieved breath. No, she wasn't crazy.

Since she'd returned, she'd taken the thing along everywhere. She even slept with it. She couldn't take a chance that her nosy roommate or the dorm parents might find it.

She thought about using it again all the time. Like maybe going back and taking tests again, after she'd gotten bad grades. Plus, she could *know* which way an opposing goalie would move and score goal after goal. She could even go back and wreck her dad's relationship with Maria. Maybe even send her dad back to be with her mom again.

Kristi leaned forward, wrapped her fingers tightly around the machine, and thought again of the horrible, impending wedding. Yes, she *could* change it.

No. She sighed and let go. She shouldn't—*couldn't*—fix her mom and dad's broken marriage, no matter how much she wanted to.

But that still didn't mean she had to like it. She let go of the time machine, leaned back, and for now only dreamed of a better world, one *without* Maria and Brittany.

1782

Ty Jordan stepped down from the crowded plank sidewalk and ran along the hard-packed dirt street. Ducking passing wagons and buggies, leaping fresh manure mines, he scanned the road and sidewalks for a glimpse of his brother. Cutting down a side street, he stepped into the path of a golden mare. Jumping aside, he narrowly missed the trampling hooves as the startled horse reared.

"Watch where you tread, nincompoop!" yelled the rider, a ponytailed man in brown knee breeches and blue wool vest. He swung a riding crop at Ty's head. "Or I'll have you flogged!"

Ty ducked, felt the braided leather swish past his ear, and hopped back onto the wooden sidewalk.

"Sorry, sir." He bowed slightly, then moved away, merging into the stream of other pedestrians. At the next street, he stepped up onto a wooden crate, pushed brown bangs from his eyes, and scanned the broad square. Men thronged the space, garbed in vests, smocks, and loose-fitting linen shirts. Some were clad in round-brimmed black hats and black waistcoats that looked too hot for the baking sun. Others wore straw hats or no hats at all. Many were accompanied by women in long white high-waisted dresses with bodices of blue, green, or brown, and ruffled mobcaps.

But Thomas was nowhere to be found.

Ty swore and jumped down. He and Thomas had left the farm for Philadelphia with their surrogate grandfather, Stephen, long before dawn that morning. The marketplace teemed with farmers and merchants, with giggling children running between stalls of cloth and leather goods. It was as packed as Ty had ever seen it and they'd sold almost all of their peaches, sweet corn, summer wheat, and greens before midday.

In celebration, Stephen had given Ty and Thomas an hour's break and a shilling to spend on whatever their hearts desired. With a wink, Thomas had taken the shilling and scurried off into the crowd as Ty was completing a sale. The young woman Ty was dealing with carefully inspected each remaining vegetable and fruit, finally settling on a single cucumber. By the time Ty was able to escape, Thomas was long gone.

At first he'd chuckled at the prank. But after half an hour of searching through the market and all the surrounding streets, he was ready to wring his brother's neck.

This had been their first trip to Philadelphia since General Cornwallis and the bulk of the royal army in the south had surrendered at Yorktown. British forces still held New York and a few places in Canada, but their numbers dwindled with every ship returning troops and loyalists to London. Both sides seemed to feel the War for Independence was over. The infant country had vanquished her oppressors. All that remained was the formal signing of a peace treaty.

Now an electric excitement filled the city, visible on the faces of the merchants and shopkeepers.

Everywhere he turned, Ty heard men speaking of the great General Washington as if he'd descended Olympus and carried the country to freedom on his back.

Ty looked up at a crudely-sewn flag hung above the door of a tavern. The circle of stars was grayish, crooked on the faded blue background. The edges were frayed and differing shades of red and white patches made up the stripes. Still it hung proudly, like hundreds of others throughout the city, waving above shops and windows, hung atop the masts of the ships in the harbor. Some were as simple, homemade, and weathered as this one. Some torn and powder-blackened, brought home from battlefields by sons and husbands. Others were crisp and immaculate, fresh and new like the country.

To Ty, and thousands of war-weary Americans, all the flags represented one wonderful thing—freedom. The end of second-and third-class citizenship as illegitimate step-countrymen. A new start in life. Exactly what Ty had hoped for when he'd decided to stay in this place and time with Stephen instead of returning to his own time with Kristi.

Turning a corner into a breeze that smelled of fish and seaweed, he picked up his pace again, thinking Thomas may have gone down to the wharf to watch the ships unload.

Prosperous-looking brick merchant homes lined the street opposite the wharf. Men in starched white shirts and freshly sewn vests stood in front of the houses, calling out numbers, poring over ledgers. The astringent smells of whisky, the rich musk of tobacco, and the salty tang of fish hung over everything.

Ty wove past a dozen schooners and small fishing vessels, sidestepping sweaty shirtless men hauling casks, barrels, and crates. Stopping a moment, he watched two of them haul a large net from their boat and dump hundreds of shimmering, flopping fish onto the wharf.

A huge, three-masted brig sat moored a hundred meters from the shore. Half a dozen rowboats traveled to and from it, most overloaded with crates and barrels. But one, which had just tied up, carried only people. A bald, burly man with arms as big around as Ty's head hopped from the stern onto its dock. In one beefy hand he gripped a length of twisted rope, the ends frayed into four separate cords, each about a foot long with knots tied on the ends. His other hand pulled another rope. Attached to it stumbled a line of black men and women in tattered homespun burlap, metal collars clamped around their necks. Iron cuffs hung loosely from gaunt wrists. The captives shuffled from the boat one by one until ten stood in a miserable wavering line. The whites of their bloodshot eyes stood out in contrast to their dark faces.

Ty's stomach tightened.

"On with ya!" The bald sailor ordered, yanking at the rope. The train of slaves lurched forward as one. One man in the middle fell to his hands and knees, which brought the man in front of him and the woman behind down as well.

"Get up, ya scurvy dogs!" the burly man barked. He swung the hemp whip, viciously hitting the fallen with the knotted ends until they'd all regained their feet.

Ty's mouth went bone dry. He looked back toward the ship from which they'd come. There, too, a pristine American flag fluttered in the wind high above its deck.

The miserable procession passed, close enough for him to smell the putrid stink of human waste. The last male slave in the line was no older than Ty, with midnight-black skin. The boy's wild eyes met his for an instant.

Ty felt paralyzed under his hopeless, desperate gaze. A fat man with wild red hair stepped from one of the buildings opposite and approached the wretched group, picking his teeth as if he'd just finished a big meal. Thick lamb-chop sideburns spread down his cheeks, bracketing a bushy, walrus mustache. His ruffled shirt was half un-tucked from low-hanging britches. The buttons of his blue vest strained to contain his fat stomach. He strolled down the line of slaves, fingering their arms and looking into the mouths of some as one would check a horse's teeth. He nodded after inspecting some, shook his head and spat after eyeing others.

At the end of the line, he stopped and tossed a little round purse to the bald sailor. The sailor led the slaves roughly through an open door in one tall red brick building. Ty caught the gaze of the young slave again. His sight of the tears rolling down the boy's face was cut off as the door slammed shut.

Ty bent and threw up on the wharf, splashing the fine leather shoes of the fat merchant.

* * *

Hours later, as the wagon bumped along the road home under a star-speckled sky, Ty lay with his head on a sack of flour in the back of the wagon among the butter, sugar, and rolls of blue fabric Miss Martha, Stephen's wife, had requested. He stared through the twilit trees, trying not to see the shiny tears in the young slave-boy's eyes in the twinkling stars.

After leaving the wharf, he'd found a chuffed Thomas waiting on a corner with two bags of sugared almonds, Ty's favorite. But Ty's stomach had been too queasy to eat, and that queasiness still hadn't left him.

Now Thomas sat on the front bench with Stephen. The two had been reveling in the day's sales success since they'd left the city. But Ty had remained apart. He couldn't get the image of the slave-boy's despairing eyes from his mind.

Two days earlier, he'd walked through their own fields—land he'd helped sow, cultivate, and reap. He'd worked hard and even felt good about the fatigue. He was working to benefit his adopted family, his adopted country. Their crops had already helped feed the armies, helped keep the revolutionary fires burning. But seeing those chained slaves herded from the ship like cattle, far from their own native soil, put a taint on the whole idea of a new, *free* country.

"Hey. You awake, brother?" Thomas called back.

Ty lifted his head. "Yeah."

"Come on up here, then."

He let out a long breath, pushed up and climbed over the back of the bench to plop down next to Thomas.

Thomas nudged him. "What're you doing back there?"

"Just...thinking."

"What about, son?" Stephen asked. Nearing sixty, he wore a silvery beard and white hair that hung to his shoulders from under a straw hat. He, too, was a transplant to the eighteenth century, sent back from 1997, when he was twenty, by the same man who'd brought Ty back.

"I saw a ship unloading slaves at the wharf. An American ship. One was just a kid, younger than you and me, Thomas. Scared out of his mind."

"Ahh." Stephen ran a hand down his beard.

Ty shook his head. "I just don't understand. How can we talk about a human right to freedom and independence out of one side of our mouths and then justify taking away someone else's freedom and independence from the other side?"

"It's beyond logic and my understanding as well, Ty," Stephen said. "Slavery has left a stain on every land throughout human history. There's mention of it in the Bible. Some governments and men use those verses to justify the skin trade, as if God gave them the right."

"But *this* government is supposed to be different," Thomas added. "It's supposed to guarantee freedom for all."

"What about that boy?" Ty insisted. "Doesn't he get any rights?"

Stephen sighed. "Slavery's a wound that will fester in the heart of this country for another eighty years, degrading master and slave both. It will take hundreds of thousands of boys losing their lives in yet another bloody war to close that wound. Then another hundred years before any real healing begins."

Ty stomped on the wooden plank beneath his feet. "That's not good enough. I should've done something back there. I should have helped them."

Stephen smiled and touched his shoulder. "You know that's too dangerous, son. We're visitors to this time, no matter how long we stay. We cannot interfere in events like that. The results could be disastrous."

"But we interfere every day by just *being* here!" Ty cried. "We just sold crops to dozens of buyers. We bought goods from others. Isn't that a sort of interfering? And what about you? You certainly *interfered* with events when you—a man from the future—married Miss Martha. But the world didn't come to an end."

Stephen's face fell. He turned away and gazed out above the horses' backs. "That's where you're wrong." He took a deep breath. "I *did* interfere when I married

14

her. I was young and didn't understand then what I do now. The son we brought into the world, our Joshua? He didn't belong here. And so he died, cold and alone, suffering along a snowy road from Valley Forge. That's what interfering brought us—what it brought our son."

TWO

Kristi slung her backpack over one shoulder and stepped from the train. The station, if you could even seriously call it that, was just a long cement slab in a gully between two steep, vine-covered hills. Men and women hurried to board or debark from the train, clutching briefcases, wheeling luggage, talking on cell phones.

Kristi scanned the waiting faces on the platform. None belonged to her father.

"Kristine! Kristine!" a high voice called. "Over here, baby girl!"

A large woman in a flowery peach dress stood up from a bench on the platform and waved both arms like a groupie hoping to be noticed by a guitarist on stage. Fighting back a groan, Kristi forced a smile and waved back. The woman rushed up with arms extended and crashed into her with a bear hug, crushing the air from her lungs. Kristi's feet left the ground as the woman swung her from side to side like a child's toy.

"Hi Aunt Deb," Kristi wheezed.

"Oh, baby girl! I missed you *so* much!" Aunt Deb eased up enough for Kristi to drop unsteadily to her feet. Knowing what was coming next, she tried to sidestep, but her aunt's hands clamped on either side of her face like a vise. Puckered red lips smacked Kristi's forehead, cheeks, nose, and finally her tightly pressed lips.

"I can't hardly believe how big you got, baby girl."

Kristi wriggled from her aunt's grip and staggered backwards, wiping her face on one sleeve. "I'm not a baby, Aunt Deb! I'm almost thirteen, you know."

"Oh, pshhh." Deb waved one hand. "You'll *always* be my baby girl."

"Where's my dad?"

"He stayed at Mimi's. Brittany wasn't feeling well, poor, sweet little thing. But you got me, baby girl."

So it begins, Kristi thought, rolling her eyes. "Right."

She spun on one heel and scaled up the steps to the parking lot two at a time. Aunt Deb huffed up behind her.

When they reached the top, Aunt Deb stepped around her and flung out one arm with a flourish, like a spokes model revealing a newly designed sports car. "Your chariot awaits, princess."

The golden coach was actually a tiny Smart Car with faded red paint. Dried, crusted mud was plastered around the wheel wells. Kristi shook her head, half expecting a dozen clowns to come clambering out when her aunt opened the door.

The whole car wobbled and the suspension groaned as Aunt Deb squeezed herself into the driver's seat. Kristi crammed her backpack into the narrow space behind the passenger seat and plopped down.

"And away we go," Deb sang as she turned the key. The engine whined for a second, then sputtered to life, sounding like an overheating vacuum cleaner.

Kristi spent most of the ride gazing out the window, not even pretending to listen to Aunt Deb chatter about her new diet, her old job at the post office, and the unusual amount of rainfall the area had gotten that fall.

She did feel a little guilty about ignoring her aunt. Deb was a sweet woman, if a little grabby and over-affectionate. But right now Kristi's stomach was in knots. Why hadn't her father come to pick her up, at least? She couldn't push down the feeling that her soon-to-be stepsister had already stolen him away.

Forty-five minutes later, Auntie turned off the highway and onto a gravel lane. They followed the twisted drive until a big two-story farmhouse came into view, an old place with stone siding and a long porch that wrapped the front and side of the house. White pillars braced the corners of the porch and bracketed broad wooden steps leading to the front door. Cars lined the yard on either side of the drive.

Deb pulled between a Mercedes and a Ford pickup. "We have arrived," she sang. "Just in time for supper, too. I'm famished."

Kristi finally looked over at her. "Thanks for coming to get me, Aunt Deb."

She grabbed her backpack, took a deep breath, and got out. A dozen of her relatives were sitting on swings and rocking chairs on the front porch, sipping iced tea, laughing and talking. But her dad wasn't one of them.

"Kristi!" called an excited voice. A young man leapt from one porch swing, galloped down the stairs, and grabbed her up in a big hug. "About time, little sister!"

"Hi, Derek," Kristi said, squeezing back. "Or should I say, *Dr. Derek?*"

He grinned. "That's Dr. Connors to you, young lady. How's school? How was your trip?"

"All right, I guess." She shrugged. "Got a detailed rundown on the crazy weather here, plus a whole concert of Auntie Deb singing Miley Cyrus and Chumbawamba."

"What fun for you." Derek winked and they both laughed. He laid a hand on her shoulder. "Come on, Mimi's been asking for you."

Kristi stepped up on the porch and into a mob of hugs and kisses. She shrugged and smiled at the many proclamations of how big she'd gotten, and slowly made her way through the crowd. Her great-grandmother sat on an antique swing at the far end of the porch, her ever-present knitting laid across her lap. Wisps of white hair peeked out from the green kerchief on Mimi's head. A matching shawl covered thin, frail shoulders. That dark, weathered face had wrinkles upon wrinkles, but the old woman's brown eyes shone with life and good humor.

"Hi, Mimi!" Kristi bent for a hug.

"Oh, Kristine. Your Mimi's so happy to see you!" She patted Kristi's back with thin fingers, then kissed her forehead. "Now we're almost complete."

Kristi turned back to Derek. "Hey, where's Sis?"

"Sarah couldn't make it."

"What?" Kristi crossed her arms. "But...if she didn't have to come, why did I?"

The other relatives on the porch suddenly found interesting things on the wall or out in the yard to look at.

Derek shrugged. "Come on. Dad's inside with Maria and Brittany."

Icy prickles ran down Kristi's spine. "That's all right. I'll wait out here until they're gone."

"Sorry, kid. No can do." He grabbed her arm and pulled the screen door open. Its hinges creaked, as if voicing Kristi's complaints. "Come on and get it over with."

He led her through the foyer and past a long table set with platters of cheese, sandwich meats, and cookies. Kristi's stomach growled, but Derek pulled her past the food and on into the living room. She dragged her feet enough to let him know she was going under protest.

At the opening of the living room, he turned to look at her. "You could *try* to smile, ya know. Dad's excited to see you."

She snorted. "Yeah, right. Just not excited enough to leave the *drama queen's* side."

Derek sighed and patted her shoulder. Then they stepped into the room where they'd spent so many Christmases back when their mother and father were still married. Small electric candles glowed through the sheer curtains in each window. Mimi's antique spinning wheel sat in one corner next to the fireplace. Kristi glanced up at the old Swiss cuckoo clock on the mantle, its face carved to resemble a log with twigs wrapped around like fingers holding it in place. Two tiny doves, so life-like Kristi used to expect them to fly off, sat perched on twigs jutting from either side of the clock face.

She felt a pang in her stomach. Her mom *loved* that old clock. When Kristi was little, the two of them used to watch it near the hour, holding their breath, then fall to the floor giggling when the little brown bird finally poked out, peeping and flapping its tiny wings.

Mimi's father, a clockmaker, had carved the cuckoo over a hundred years earlier. Kristi's mom had always joked about inheriting it someday. The pang in Kristi's stomach sharpened. Maria would probably get it now. The new, favorite granddaughter.

And there, across the room, stood her dad. A big man, tall and stocky. He'd played football for two years in college before deciding on law school. His stomach was a little rounder now, his hair a little grayer. Fine lines creased the corners of his eyes and framed his mouth like parentheses. He leaned over the couch on which Brittany was lying.

Maria knelt on the hardwood floor next to the girl. Ok, sure—the woman *was* beautiful. Kristi couldn't deny that. That soft, olive-brown skin so smooth, the eyes a sparkling jade, that thick, wavy hair, a glossy black, not one strand out of place.

But Kristi saw through that disguise. The woman was a siren, like the ancient ones that had enchanted Odysseus with their songs in that book she read for English class. Of course her dad—a lawyer, not a Greek warrior—would be powerless against the witch's devilish charms.

"Special delivery," Derek announced.

James Connors looked up and his face lit. *"There's* my princess!" He crossed the room in three long strides, wrapped his arms around Kristi, and lifted her up in the traditional family bear-hug.

For half a heartbeat, Kristi forgot her anger. The rest of the world faded away and suddenly she was a little girl again, safe and happy in her dad's strong arms. She closed her eyes and laid her cheek on his shoulder. "Hi, Daddy."

"Did you have a good trip?" His deep voice rumbled.

She nodded. After a few seconds, he loosened his grip and she slid back to her feet.

Then Maria stepped toward her with that big, fake smile and all the anger washed back into Kristi like a tsunami.

"Hello, Kristine." Maria touched Kristi's shoulder with soft, well-manicured fingers. "We're so happy you've come to celebrate with us."

21

Kristi jerked her shoulder back as if Maria's hand were contagious. "Like I had a choice," she muttered.

"What was that, dear?" Maria frowned slightly.

But her dad's shoulders had stiffened. He'd gotten the gist of her words, at least. Kristi lowered her head and mumbled, "Nothing."

Maria took her hand. "Come say hi to Brittany. She's so excited to see her big sister."

"Can't wait," Kristi said, avoiding her dad's hurt eyes.

Ten-year-old Brittany's short, plump frame only took up half the over-stuffed couch. She was wearing a puffy red dress and white tights, looking like a lollipop on two sticks. A wet washcloth covered her eyes and forehead.

"Momma, my head hurts," the girl whined.

"I know, darling," crooned Maria. "Here, say hello to your big sister."

She's NOT my sister, Kristi screamed in her head, even as she made her mouth say, "Hey, Brittany."

"I don't *want* to say hello!" the girl protested.

Kristi bit her lip. *Oh, yeah? Well me neither, Bub!*

Maria blushed and bit her lip. "Oh, don't be such a gloomy Gus, darling. Just say hi."

Brittany huffed. She lifted the cold compress just enough for a shadowed sliver to appear over one eye. "Hi."

"There," Maria said, petting her hair. "That was nice."

Yeah, Kristi thought. *Nice as a snakebite.*

"Come on," her dad said, grasping her shoulder. "We'll let Brittany get some rest."

Derek left to go back outside and Kristi followed her father through the swinging door and into the kitchen.

More party trays of meats, cheeses, veggies, pickles, and olives lined the granite kitchen countertops.

"Hungry?" her dad asked.

Her stomach growled loudly, but Kristi shook her head. Darned if she'd eat any of this food and join the *celebration*.

Her dad motioned her over to a seat at the round table pushed next to the wall, then poured himself a mug of coffee. They sat across, neither looking at the other. There were so many things Kristi wanted to say, so many complaints she wanted to register. But she kept her mouth closed, staring at the same cream-colored behemoth of a refrigerator that had sat in that same corner since her father was a kid.

When she finally looked back at him, he wasn't smiling anymore. Deep lines creased his forehead. He opened his mouth—once, twice—but closed it again without saying anything. She could've laughed. Here was Philadelphia's most feared trial lawyer, tongue-tied and sweating, as if he was trying to figure out how to explain boys and kissing to her all over again.

She took a deep breath and delivered the first blow. "Where's Sarah?"

His jaw tightened. He shrugged one shoulder. "She's researching for a big case and couldn't get away."

"Come on, Dad." Kristi leaned forward. "You expect me to believe that?"

"I don't know what to expect anymore, Kristi." He sighed and ran a hand over his thinning hair. "She's having a tough time with this, too. I know what you're thinking, what you're feeling. You'll understand better when you're old—"

"In case you haven't noticed, I'm not a little kid anymore!" She felt her face heating. "You *don't* know how I'm feeling. I'm *never* going to understand. This is like kicking Mom in the gut, you know."

"But your mother has a boyfriend, too," he sputtered.

"It doesn't matter. You threw her away first so you could, what? Marry that...*woman*." She pointed a rigid finger toward the other room.

Now his face flushed hotly. "That *woman* is going to be your step-mother starting tomorrow, Kristine."

"No, Dad. Maybe she's going to be your wife, but never my step-mom. I have a *real* mother. I don't need her or her whiny brat of a daughter."

He slammed a fist onto the table, rattling the dishes so hard coffee sloshed out of his mug. Kristi didn't flinch. "Now you listen here, young lady! If you think—"

Mimi pushed into the kitchen just then and he fell silent. The old woman crossed the room, thumping her cane on the linoleum at each step. Her dad sat back and crossed his arms. Kristi did the same.

"I hate to break up the happy reunion, but your Mimi needs a hand getting to her room. Would you mind, Kristine, dear?"

"Yes, Mimi. I'll help you up."

"Bring yourself a plate of food too, honey."

"I'm not hungry."

Mimi's thin eyebrows raised. "I don't recall asking if you were, girl. Now get something to eat and come this way without any more sass."

"Yes, Mimi," Kristi said meekly, avoiding looking in her father's direction.

She went to the counter and threw a few carrots, some sliced turkey, and a roll onto a paper plate. Her father's chair scraped the linoleum. His big hand touched her back lightly. "I *am* glad you're here, Kristi."

She nodded without taking her eyes off the food. After a moment he left the kitchen and Kristi took one of Mimi's thin arms and led her up the stairs.

Mimi's bedroom was larger than the family room. Her bed, big enough to swallow such a small, frail woman, sat under a wide window that showed the sky darkening outside. A bookcase filled one wall, its shelves packed with photo albums, bibles, and old books with cracked, leather spines. Histories and biographies, children's picture books, hardcover novels spanning a hundred years. Three or four long shelves were devoted to Mimi's guilty passion, paperback romances. Kristi and her cousins used to sneak up here and giggle at the cover illustrations of shirtless, muscle-bound men kissing women in sheer, revealing gowns.

Opposite the bookcase stood a stone fireplace, Mimi's antique rocking chair, and a wicker basket piled high with a multitude of colored yarns and different sized wooden knitting needles.

Mimi eased down into the rocker, picked out a pair, and laid out a partially-made yellow blanket across her lap. She started in on it, clacking the needles together with the deftness of fingers fifty years younger.

Kristi sat on the stone ledge of the fireplace and set the plate of food beside her.

"Eat up," Mimi said. "I know you're hungry."

Kristi picked up a baby carrot and nibbled on it.

"How you doing, girl?" Mimi asked without looking up from her work.

"Great. Never better."

Now her great-grandmother looked up, but the clacking didn't slow an instant. "Don't you lie to your Mimi, girl."

Kristi rolled her eyes. "I'd be *fine* if Dad didn't treat me like such a child."

Mimi laughed. "You *are* a child, child. Don't be in such a rush to grow up."

"Don't worry. He won't *ever* let me."

"He means well, Kristine. He knows this is hard on you. But Maria is part of his life now. And Brittany, too.

So if you still want to be, too, you're going to have to accept that."

Tears stung Kristi's eyes. She blinked, willing herself not to cry, not to care. But they burned hot streaks down her face anyway. "How can I, when what he's doing betrays my mom?"

Mimi smiled. "I love your momma, Kristine. You know that. And she's a strong woman. You being here for your father isn't a betrayal. It's a family thing. She understands that."

Kristi sniffled and wiped her face with the back of one hand. "Mom says she doesn't even care anymore. She's been taking pottery classes and joined a book club. She never did stuff like that when they were married."

"She's moving on, girl. Being better to her own self. You could do the same, if you'd only let yourself."

Kristi shrugged one shoulder.

"Go on over and get that old family album from the shelf," Mimi said. "I want to show you something."

Kristi went to the shelves. A dozen photo albums lined the bottom. "Which one?"

"That fat one right there." Mimi pointed to the far end.

Kristi spied a large, faded leather album with worn edges and a narrow, frayed ribbon hanging from the binding. "This old one?"

"That's it. Bring it here."

When she pulled it out of the shelf it dropped to the floor like dead weight. "Geez, Mimi. How can you even lift this thing?"

The old woman winked. "Your Mimi's still got some strength in these old bones."

Kristi brought it over and set it gently on the old woman's lap.

"This, my girl, is our family history." Mimi leafed through some pages and opened to a picture of Kristi's parents on their wedding day, standing hand-in-hand. "There your momma is, and there she'll stay. She's still a part of this family."

Kristi ran a finger over the picture. Her father towered over his bride, as he did most people. The contrasts between the two were startling. While his skin was deep brown, almost black, her mother's was a fairer, mocha color. She was beaming. Her eyes sparkled. But his face was stoic, serious. Her brilliant white dress next to his black tuxedo made them look like complete opposites. Funny, they didn't look like they belonged together, even back then.

"Here's some of you kids." Mimi flipped to another page. It held pictures of a younger Derek. In one, from middle school, his hair stood straight up and the high fade made it look like he had a fuzzy box sitting on his head.

Sarah was on the opposite page. Some school pictures, too, and a few from concerts back when she'd played the clarinet. One from her prom night, when she'd worn a tight, sparkling blue dress. Kristi had been too young to remember that night, but she'd heard of the trouble Sarah had gotten into for skipping curfew and staying out all night.

"I didn't know you kept all these," she said.

She flipped farther on, until she found her own page, with pictures of her at basketball. Then a newspaper clipping about her playing for an all-star soccer team two years earlier. She'd traveled with her dad to Montana for that tournament, just the two of them. They'd stayed in a hotel, eaten pizza for dinner each night, and stayed up late laughing through corny old movies. An ache formed in her chest. She flipped away from those pictures, toward the front of the book, past photos of her dad and Aunt Deb when they were little. She stopped at an old, yellowed portrait of another beautiful woman in a wedding gown. Standing next to her was a tall man in a brown aviator's uniform. "Who's this?"

"Why, that's me and Poppy, your great-granddaddy."

Kristi's eyes widened. She glanced between the ancient woman and the beautiful, young vibrant one in the picture. "That's *you?*"

"I wasn't always old and decrepit." Mimi chuckled. "Used to have gentlemen callers beating down my door, trying to get past my daddy to take me out. You should've seen him chasing boys away with a pitchfork. And you think *your* daddy's tough!"

"But he didn't chase Poppy away?"

"Yes ma'am, he sure did. Half a dozen times. But my James was as stubborn as you and your daddy put together. He kept coming back, week after week. Finally, just before your Poppy left for the war, my daddy gave him permission to send me letters. We wrote back and forth every week for two long years. He wrote the most beautiful letters and poems. We married two weeks after he got home."

"I wish I could've met him," Kristi said.

"Oh, he would've loved you, girl. I've never met a man with a bigger heart." Mimi touched her husband's photo and sighed. "Here, look at this." She flipped to the beginning of the album and carefully slid a stiff, yellowed parchment from the front pocket. She unfolded and spread it over the album. It was over two feet wide, filled with dozens of handwritten names, all branching from two at the top: Jonah and Celia Connors. Mimi pointed to those. "Your poppy's granddaddy started this record back in 1870. Poppy kept it going and I've kept it up since he passed. Your daddy will have it someday. Then if you want, maybe you'll keep it up after that."

Kristi marveled as she traced a finger along the lines of her ancestors, most of which she didn't recognize. She found her dad and mom, then Derek, Sarah, and herself, with blank spots left for future spouses. She chuckled, wondering what name would someday be written next to hers, what children would branch from her line. She ran a finger up the line to her great-great-great grandfather, Jonah Connors. In a horizontal line from his name was a lone name, Britt Connors. This one had a birth date, 1850, but no date of death. No wife listed, no children branching below.

"Who's this?" Kristi asked, touching the name.

"That's Jonah's brother, Britt. Your poppy's daddy was named for him."

"What happened? Didn't he get married?"

Mimi shook her head. "Nobody knows. Jonah and Britt grew up together on a plantation in Maryland."

She gasped at her grandmother. "*Plantation*? You mean...they were *slaves*?"

Mimi nodded. "Neither one knew who their mothers or fathers were, so they called themselves brothers. They ran away from the plantation together and made their way north. But Britt was caught by slave catchers and never heard from again. He was only eight. Jonah wound up in a Quaker community, where they set him up to meet Harriet Tubman. Mrs. Tubman took him the rest of the way to Canada, where he met Celia and they stayed until after the Civil War."

"Harriet Tubman! *The* Harriet Tubman!" Kristi cried. "She helped *my* great-great-great grandfather escape from slavery?"

Mimi smiled. "They called her Moses, you know, leading her people to the Promised Land. Never lost a soul to the slave catchers."

"Wow! That's so cool!" She touched Britt's name again. "Too bad Harriet couldn't have helped him, too."

"Have a look at this." Mimi flipped to the next page. Tucked there was another piece of paper, this one even more yellowed and crumpled than the one with the family tree. On it was a faded scrawl. "These are telegraphs Jonah sent to his wife while searching down south for Britt after the war."

April, 1866
The Big House was burnt by a mob. Master Conwell went to Georgia.

May, 1866
Found Master Conwell in Atlanta. He was mad and wouldn't tell me anything about Britt. Missus said Britt never came back to the plantation.

Kristi shook her head. "That's so sad. I wonder what happened. Do you think the slave catchers killed him?"

"Hard to say," Mimi said. "But I don't think so. Slave catchers didn't get paid for killing runaways. Instead of returning him for the reward, they could've taken him south, though. Sold him for more there. But Jonah never found out." She sighed. "Kind of makes our own troubles seem trivial, doesn't it?"

Kristi nodded, suddenly feeling childish and guilty. She'd been sulking about her dad getting remarried. But her ancestors had to worry about real troubles, like slavery and lost relatives. A pit grew in her stomach as she imagined Jonah and Britt living enslaved, then running for their lives. Of Britt disappearing altogether. It was too sad to even think about.

THREE:
1782

Ty stared at the dark ceiling of his bedroom, listening to the even, sleeping breaths of Thomas in the bed next to him. He sighed and rolled over, wishing he could fall asleep, too. They'd been up since sunrise, scythed corn stalks until their arms hung limp as pasta noodles, then weeded the potato field until sundown. His body ached, begging for sleep. But his racing mind wouldn't allow it.

It'd been the same each night since he'd returned from Philadelphia. The image of the slave-boy was etched in his mind. While working, it was easier to push the memory aside, to lose himself in sweaty effort. But the boy's tortured gaze reappeared each time he slowed and tried to rest.

Who was the boy? Had he been kidnapped from the coast of Africa and transported across the sea? Or born a slave, never having tasted freedom? Where was he now? Working a plantation in Georgia? Cleaning a saloon in Charleston? Did he have a bed to sleep in or have to share a tiny, one-room shack with other slaves?

Thomas snored, then smacked his lips. Ty glared. They were the same, weren't they? Could finish each other's sentences, almost read each other's thoughts. Thomas hated slavery as much as Ty did. Stephen and Miss Martha did, too. But none of them had seen the chain of slaves or the pleading eyes of the boy. They hadn't stood helpless, watching the sad parade pass without lifting a finger to help.

Ty let out a heavy breath. He *should* have done something, no matter what Stephen said.

If only Kristi had been with him. She probably would've rushed the slaver, hit him over the head, stolen his keys, and freed the slaves. She would've acted and forced Ty to help. She wouldn't have just gawked like a frightened child.

That made him smile. Of course, Kristi's scheme wouldn't have included *how* they were to escape and avoid the hangman's noose for stealing a slave. Figuring out the *how* had always been Ty's job. Kristi was the queen of troublemaking. Ty the king of fixing that trouble so they didn't get arrested... or worse.

God, did he miss her!

He closed his eyes and felt sleep trying to numb his weary bones. Just as he started to drift off, a crash and a startled whinny came through the opened window. He sat straight up and listened hard, but no more sounds followed.

"Hey," he whispered, shaking the other boy's shoulder. "You hear that?"

Thomas groaned, rolled over, and snored again.

"Way to be a hero, brother." Ty slid from bed and opened the door. The hallway was dark. He stole down the stairs, avoiding the creaky fourth step. An oil lantern sat on the kitchen table. He lit it with a loafer and opened the front door. A warm breeze blew through his nightshirt. The full-moon shone big and bright, casting an eerie pale light over the farm.

A rustling came from the barn. One of the horses must've gotten out of its stall. Ty descended the porch steps and crossed the yard. The door was unlatched, hanging open a crack. But Stephen *always* latched the barn door. Ty pushed warily into the barn and held up the lantern to look around. All three horses stood in their stalls, gazing back at him.

"Hello?" he called.

Something shuffled across the boarding in the hayloft. Bits of hay fell through the cracks and drifted to the floor.

"Who's there?" He tried to make his voice deeper and gruffer, but it came out squeaky. Heart pattering, Ty grabbed a pitchfork from the wall. He held the lantern's handle in his mouth and climbed the ladder to the loft.

"Come out," he said, stepping onto the loft floor. He swung the lantern, revealing only bales and piles of strewn hay. "I have a gun."

"Please mista, don' shoot," answered a deep, quavering voice. "We don' mean no harm."

Ty flinched. He held the pitchfork ahead of him and cleared his throat. "Well, then—come on out."

One bale of hay shifted and a shadowed figure emerged from behind it. Ty lifted the lantern higher, illuminating a black man's face, his wide, scared eyes. He wore a filthy white shirt and torn breeches. He was barefoot.

"Please, mista," he repeated. "We's jus' lookin' foah a place ta sleep."

A child peered out from behind the man's legs. A boy, four or five years old, tears streaking his dirt-crusted face. When he caught sight of Ty, he sobbed. "He gone kill us, Papa?"

* * *

Kristi left Mimi's room and stopped at the railing to listen to the voices and laughter coming from the family room. Her dad's deep, booming tenor rose above them all.

"So this guy's robbing a bank and gets spooked. Well, he runs out with about seventy-five bucks, all quarters in a sack, but gets trapped in the vestibule. He bangs away at the door to the outside, but can't push it open. He kicks and screams, ramming the door over and over again with one shoulder. When the police arrive, he drops to his knees, crying. The cops open the door with ease. There, clear as day on the security camera, the sign on the exit door says 'Pull'."

The room erupted in laughter.

Her dad's voice cracked as he tried to continue. "This...genius kept trying to push open a door that said *pull*. Can you believe that?"

Maria's shrill cackle rose above the others. Kristi stopped herself in mid-eye roll. She'd promised Mimi she'd try harder. But was it *her* fault Maria's laugh sounded like a chipmunk who'd inhaled helium from a birthday balloon?

She continued down the hall and pushed the door to her room open. Someone was in there. Her heart constricted. Brittany stood at the foot of the bed, holding Kristi's backpack in one hand and the time machine in the other.

"Hey! What the heck are you doing in my stuff?"

Brittany jumped, skittish as a spooked cat. She spun and dropped the backpack, cradling the time rod to her chest.

"Give me that!" Kristi demanded, ripping it away.

The girl backed away, smirking. "What is it, anyway? A magic wand for the *princess*?"

Kristi stuffed the machine back into her pack. "That's right, *Brat*-ney. A magic wand. So get out of here before I turn you into a toad. Oh, wait. I forgot. You already are one."

Brittany scowled, jaw jutting out. "*You're* the slimy toad. Besides, I don't have to leave. This is my room, too."

"No way!" Kristi cried. "I'm not sharing a room with *you*!"

Brittany shrugged. "Too bad. Dad said so."

"He's *not* your dad!"

Brittany's grin widened. "He will be after tomorrow, tomorrow," she sang to the tune of that annoying song from the Annie musical. She went over to the closet and poked at the puffy blue dress hanging there. "Is *that* what you're gonna wear?" She ran the back of one hand along the frilly lace lining the sleeve. "Ha! You'll look more like a spoiled cream-puff than a princess." She took it from the hanger, held it against herself, and held out the frilly sleeve with one hand. Then she spun in a circle, humming.

"Give me that!" Kristi yanked the dress away and took it back to the closet. "Keep your toady paws off my stuff!"

The closet was shallow, barely deep enough for hangers. As Kristi reached up to put the dress away, Brittany shoved her in and slammed the door.

Kristi froze. Her heart thumped like bongo drums in her chest. Chilling sweat formed on her brow and trickled down the nape of her neck.

Once, three years earlier, she'd been playing hide-'n-seek with friends at a trash heap and had hidden inside an old refrigerator with a latched handle. She'd tried to

36

be careful not to let the door close all the way, but she'd slipped and pulled it shut. The latch had caught. She'd been trapped. And though she'd kicked and screamed herself hoarse, the door hadn't budged. She didn't remember passing out, or when a friend had found her and run to get her father. But sometimes, when she closed her eyes, she could still feel those close, coffin-like walls.

"Open the door!" She pounded on the door, screaming. "Let me out!"

"Not 'til you say *you're* the Toad Princess," Brittany sang. "Tomorrow, tomorrow..."

The closet was getting smaller. Kristi clapped her hands over her ears, then threw her body against the door. The second time it gave way and she fell out sprawled on the floor.

Brittany stepped back, eyes wide, smile faltering.

"I'm going to kill you!" Kristi roared, jumping at the younger girl.

Brittany curled into a ball on the bed, arms over her head, whimpering. Kristi stood over her, fists clenched, ready to punch her face.

Instead she took a deep breath and wiped the tears from her eyes. There, on the floor in front of the closet, lay the ripped sleeve of her fancy dress. A heavy weight dropped in her stomach. "Look what you did!"

Brittany jumped up. As she ran for the door, she laughed. "Ooops," she taunted. "Dad's going to be soooo mad you ripped your dress. Probably think you did it on purpose. Boy, are you in trouble!"

Kristi grabbed a book from the nightstand and hurled it at her head. Brittany ducked, then slammed the door and ran down the hallway, still cackling.

* * *

"Thomas," Ty whispered, leaning over his sleeping brother. "Tom, wake up."

The boy groaned and tried to roll over, to turn away. Ty got a hold of his shoulders and shook him. "*Wake up!*"

Thomas's eyes snapped open. He sat up against the headboard. "Wh—what're you doing? What's wrong?"

"Shhhhh," Ty said. "You'll wake Stephen and Martha. Come on, you gotta see this."

Thomas frowned. "It's the middle of the night. Are you mad?"

"Maybe. But come on. Or are you going to keep lying there like an idiot?"

"I'm coming, I'm coming." He threw on some trousers and followed Ty down the stairs. "Where're we going?"

"The barn."

"What? Why in the middle of the bloody night?"

"You'll see when we get there." Ty grabbed a loaf of bread and a round of cheese from the kitchen table, then led Thomas across the dusty paddock to the barn. They pushed through the door. The lantern glowed orange up at the top of the hayloft ladder.

Thomas pulled himself up after Ty. "So what's this all about?"

"Come on out," Ty whispered. "It's safe. Just me and my brother."

The man and his son came out from behind a bale of hay.

Thomas's jaw dropped. "What the—"

"Here." Ty handed them the bread and cheese. "It's all I have now, but I'll bring more later."

"Gawd bless you, suh," the man said, breaking off a hunk of bread and handing it to his son. The boy dropped to his knees and tore into the simple fare like a starved puppy. He was a tiny creature, face sunken, arms no bigger around than a sapling.

"What is this, Ty?" Thomas asked. "Where did they come from?"

"V'ginia," the man mumbled around a mouthful of bread. "My name's Cyrus. This here's m' boy, Xander."

"Are you—slaves?" Thomas asked.

Cyrus stiffened and stepped in front of his son. "We ain' lookin' for no problems, young massa."

"No, no, no." Ty waved his arms. "Don't worry. You're safe here. Nobody's going to turn you in."

Cyrus unclenched his jaw, then sat abruptly next to his son. Ty and Thomas sat in front of them.

"I gots my free papers," Cyrus said, biting off another hunk of bread. "Earned 'em fightin' agin' da British. Made me some extra money smithin' foah some officers, jus' like I did for Massa. One say he gonna give me work in Boston afta da war iffin I could make my way up der. But I went back for my boy, firs'. Massa got real angry. Tol' me ta stay on wit him, even though I be free, now. When I says no, he say he gonna sell my boy down south." Cyrus slammed a fist on the board beneath him. "I ain' gonna let my son suffer chains no more. So I jus' took 'im dat night and went north. Dey been chasin' us all da way. We's goin' ta Boston where we ken bot' be free."

Ty's head throbbed. He glanced at the skinny little boy. What kind of monster would sell a child?

"Stay as long as you need," he said. "You're safe up here. We'll bring you food and water."

"Gawd bless ya, little massas," Cyrus said. Tears welled in his eyes.

"Don't call us that," Ty said quickly. "I'm Ty. This is my brother, Thomas."

Cyrus nodded. "Gawd bless bot' of you."

Thomas nodded. "Maybe Stephen can take them to Philadelphia, get them on a ship to Boston."

"No, we can't tell Stephen," Ty said. "We're not supposed to *interfere*, remember?"

"But this is different," Thomas said. "He wouldn't just stand by when they're right here asking for help, would he?"

"I don't know." Ty sighed. "I just don't know."

* * *

Kristi sat on the bed. The ripped dress lay across her lap. Of course her father would think she'd done it on purpose. There's no way he'd believe it'd been precious little Brittany's fault. She wouldn't, if she were him.

She wished Ty were here with her. He'd know what to do. But no, he'd abandoned her, stayed back in the past, left her alone when she needed him most. He was probably—

Of course—that was the answer! She had the time machine. She could go back in time and stop Brittany from locking her in the closet. Then, the dress wouldn't be ripped up. She dug the time machine from her bag and held it out in front of her. She only needed to go back fifteen minutes, burst in on Brittany while her other self was still in Mimi's room, and get the dress out of there.

She started pushing buttons. The blue and red lights flashed along its length. She could do this little trip on her own. No big deal.

Then she thought of Mimi. *Kind of makes our own problems seem trivial, doesn't it?* Trivial problems. Like a ripped dress.

Laughing at herself, Kristi turned the time machine off. She was being selfish. Again. To risk everything by going back in time, and for what? A stupid dress. What if something went wrong? She could end up trapped a thousand years ago. Or flash back again and land in the middle of the living room, with a dozen of her relatives staring in amazement. Or in Mimi's room with her other self. Good luck explaining that one!

She stuffed the time machine back and put the bag on her shoulder. She grabbed the dress, glanced up and down the hallway, then bolted for Mimi's room and knocked. Heavy footfalls were thumping up the stairs. When Mimi opened the door, Kristi pushed past and closed it behind her.

"Sorry, Mimi," she gasped, holding up the dress, showing the ripped sleeve. "But I need your help."

Mimi frowned and tsked. "Girl, please. What did you do?"

"It wasn't me. Brittany locked me in the closet."

Mimi propped her hands on her hips, eyebrows rising.

"Mimi, I *swear* it was an accident. But Dad'll never believe it. He's going to kill me!"

"You're going to be the end of me." Her great-grandmother sighed, then took the dress.

"Thanks, Mimi. You're the best!"

"I've heard that one before." Mimi eased into her rocking chair, dug thread and a needle from her basket, and set to work.

"Can I look at the album again?" Kristi asked.

Mimi nodded, so she pulled it off the shelf and lugged it to Mimi's bed. She spread out the family tree again and touched her mom's name.

"Are you going to add Maria to this, too?"

Mimi nodded. "I expect so."

"But not Brittany, right? I mean, it's not like she's *really* family."

Mimi shot her a hard look, but didn't answer.

Kristi turned back to the parchment. The name of Britt Connors drew her eye again. What had happened to the boy? He was just a kid. Why'd he have to get caught? Why couldn't he have gone free like Jonah?

She glanced down at her backpack on the floor, thought about the time machine hidden inside, and chuckled. Now *that* would be a reason to go back in time again. Not for some stupid problem like a dress, but to go back and find Britt Connors. To help somebody *else.*

"Mimi, when did Jonah and Britt run away?"

"Some time in the spring of 1858, I think."

"Where did they live? I mean, before they ran away? Where was the plantation?"

"Near Chestertown, Maryland. Why?"

Kristi shrugged, but an excitement was sprouting in her chest. She knew where and when the boys would be. Why *couldn't* she go back and find them. Her heart was suddenly racing. She bit her lip. "I'll—I'll be right back. I have to—a—do something."

Mimi set the sewing down and eyed her sharply. "What are you scheming, Kristine?"

"Nothing." She gave her best sweet, innocent smile. *If only you knew...* She grabbed her backpack and raced from the room, back to her own. Brittany hadn't returned yet.

She locked the door, drew the time rod from her bag and lit it up again. Red and blue lights sparkled up and down the length. She typed *Chestertown: Maryland: January: 1: 1858* onto the screen. If she arrived well before their escape attempt, she'd have time to figure out a way to help.

She bent the rod into a halo and the blinking lights flashed. Just before the ends met, an image of Ty's stern face, as if he were admonishing her for some wrong, flashed into her head. She took a deep breath and let the rod straighten again.

Slow down, she told herself, chuckling as she thought how, if Ty were here, he'd be telling her not to be rash. *Think this through.* She was a twelve-year-old black girl, about to drop herself into the slavery-dominated south of a hundred and fifty years ago, aiming to help two slaves escape, on her own. But what if she were caught? Who would help *her*?

She turned the machine off and fell back onto the bed. No, it was impossible. She imagined Ty again, shaking his head. "I know, I know," she grumbled. "'Don't be rash!'"

Wait a minute. Ty! He could help her. She powered the machine up again. This time, she typed *DARBY: PENNSYLVANIA, JULY: 17: 1782*.

Taking a deep breath, she bent the rod again. Sure this time, she touched the ends together, making the required halo. Wind roared from the center as the metal heated. The sheets on the bed fluttered, the curtains blew back. The lamp next to the bed flickered, then dimmed. The flashing lights of the halo cast her shadow weirdly on the walls.

"Here goes," she said, lowering the halo. Warm metal grazed her forehead and suddenly she was rocketed forward through ribbons of white light, then spun round and round as if caught in the spin cycle of a washing machine. A whining roar blared in her ears. Painful pressure built in her head. When she opened her mouth to scream, nothing came out. A wave of nausea crashed through her, then—everything went black.

FOUR

Ty sat in the kitchen at the long pine table, elbows propped on the top, chin resting on his hands. He stifled a yawn and rubbed his eyes, feeling as though he were hovering outside his body and watching the world through blurry glass. The hour of sleep he'd managed before dawn seemed to have actually made him feel worse than no sleep at all.

Thomas sat across, head propped on his hands as well. His thin face was pale and drawn. Dark circles shadowed his eyes. Portly Miss Martha moved about the kitchen, humming as she stirred a black kettle hanging in the fireplace. She cut two pieces of bread from a large loaf and slid them in front of Ty and Thomas.

"Now don't you two look like death rolled over." She tsked, rolled up one sleeve, and touched Ty's forehead with thick fingers. "Are you coming down with the grippe?"

"Just a little tired," Ty said.

She clicked her tongue again. "That husband of mine. He's working you to the bone!" She went to the fireplace, returned with a metal pitcher, and poured steaming coffee into their tin mugs. "I've told him before: growing boys need more rest."

Ty blew across the surface of the coffee before taking a sip. He winced as the hot, bitter brew singed his lip, but it made him feel a little more awake. He smiled at Martha. "We can't complain. Stephen works harder than the two of us put together."

"Where is Stephen, anyhow?" Thomas grinned. "The old man's not sleeping in, is he?"

She laughed. "Stephen Haines won't sleep in 'til he's planted in the ground himself. He's out in the barn, I think. Why not go tell him the coffee's ready?"

Ty met a panicked glance from Thomas. He slammed his mug down, sloshing coffee onto the tabletop. Thomas knocked his chair over as he jumped up. They raced from the kitchen and across the yard.

When they burst into the barn, Stephen was just setting foot on the first rung of the ladder, a pitchfork in hand.

"Stephen!" Thomas yelled. "What are you doing?"

The farmer flinched and turned to look. "Just getting some hay for the stalls. Why?"

"I—I'll do it!" Ty blurted. He rushed over and tried to grab the pitchfork.

Stephen pulled it away. "I'm perfectly capable of climbing a ladder, Ty. Go fill the water trough if you want to help out."

"No, really Stephen. You know Miss Martha doesn't like you climbing up to the hayloft."

"Yeah," Thomas added. "She sent us out to—to get you. Coffee's ready."

Stephen looked back and forth between them, eyes narrowed. "What are you up to?"

"Nothing." Ty finally tugged the pitchfork from Stephen's grasp and pushed past him, onto the ladder.

"All right, suit yourselves." Stephen shrugged. "Toss down three or four bales, and then water the horses.

Meet me in the cornfield when you're done. I'm off for a hot cup of coffee." He wiped his hands on his pants and left the barn.

"Whoa." Thomas let out a long breath. "That was too close."

"Tell me about it." Ty shook his head. "How long do you think we're going to have to keep him out of here?"

Thomas shrugged. "Couldn't say. I'll go water the horses."

Ty climbed up to the loft. Cyrus and Xander were in a gap between bales, the boy lay on the hard bare planks, sleeping. Cyrus sat beside him, eyes wide, forehead sheened with sweat.

"You all right?" Ty asked.

Cyrus nodded. "We's fine. We'll git on outta here come sundown. Won't be no more trouble ta you den."

"No, you're no trouble," Ty said. "Don't worry about Stephen. We can keep him out of—"

"Hullo, there!" called a strange voice from outside the barn.

Ty crawled over the planks to peer through a space between the boards. His breath caught. Two men on horseback waited in front of the corral. Ty recognized the bushy white mustache of the Darby sheriff, his black hat and coat. He didn't know the other man, a stranger far dirtier than the sheriff. A fierce-looking one with eyes mere slits in a leathery, unshaven face. Ty's breath caught. Both men had muskets in sling holsters on their saddles.

"Stay right here and be quiet," Ty whispered to Cyrus. He crawled by him and swung down the ladder. When he hit the floor, he sidled to the door and peeked through.

Now Stephen was on the porch, Miss Martha right behind him. His face looked calm, but lines of worry creased Martha's brow. Thomas came up behind Stephen and kept glancing toward the barn.

"Quit looking over here!" Ty growled through his teeth.

"We're looking for a couple o' runaway Negros, Mr. Haines," the sheriff said. "They were spotted in Chester day before last, headin' this way."

"Don't know anything about that, Samuel," Stephen said.

"I'm sure you don't, Stephen. But you wouldn't mind us lookin' around the farm, would you?"

Thomas's panicked gaze fell on the barn again, then he stared up at Stephen, as if pleading.

Stephen patted the boy's head. "Actually, I would, Samuel. We're busy with harvesting and getting ready for the market. You come in for a cup of coffee if you like. Martha just brewed a fresh pot. But there are no contraband slaves here. You've no cause to search my property."

The sheriff grunted as he swung down, took off his hat, and wiped his brow with a white handkerchief. "You know I don't care much for chasin' runaways, Stephen. But the law's the law and Mr. Ratney here has been charged by his employer to find some lost property."

Ratney spat in the dirt. "And if'n y'all don't got nuthin' ta hide, then there ain't no reason for us not to look 'round a bit."

Stephen crossed his arms. "You're welcome to a cup coffee as well, Mr. Ratney. But I'm not going to stand for *my* private property being searched because someone else got careless and lost his *property*." He sneered as he said the word *property*, as if the word tasted bad on his tongue.

A heavy thump came from behind Ty. He looked over one shoulder and saw Cyrus standing in the loft, Xander in his arms. He'd knocked a hay bale over when he lifted his son.

"What was that?" Ratney swung down from his saddle and reached for his musket.

"Calm down, sir," Stephen said. "My grandson is in the barn moving hay for the stock." He cupped his hands around his mouth and called, "Come on out here, Ty."

Ty waited a moment, as if taking time to climb down from the loft. He mouthed, *get down,* to Cyrus, then stepped out and closed the door behind him.

"What is it, Grandpa?"

"Have you seen any sign of runaways about?" Stephen asked.

Ty screwed his face up. "Runaways?" He forced a laugh. "Who'd want to run way out here?"

"Whatcha doin' in there, boy?" Ratney nodded at the barn. "Ain't hidin' nobody, is you?"

"What?" Ty's mouth dropped open. "No sir—I—"

"Mr. Ratney." Stephen stepped down from the porch, frowning. "I'd be obliged for you to address your questions to me, sir, and not badger my grandson."

One of the horses whinnied from inside the barn.

Ratney grinned savagely. "Not hidin' anyone, eh?" He pushed past Ty.

"No," Ty grabbed at his sleeve. "That was just my horse."

Ratney pushed his hand off and stepped over to the barn doors. "Come on out, now. No trouble, now."

But when Ratney reached for the door it burst open, knocking him to the dirt. Cyrus rode Foxe out into the yard, Xander seated in front of him, clinging to the horse's mane. He took off down the drive at the gallop.

"Git after 'em, Sheriff!" Ratney screamed as he scrambled to his feet.

The sheriff crossed his arms. "I'm too old to gallop off after a man and run him down like a dog. I agreed to help you search, and I did. You want him, go on and get him yourself."

Ratney swore, climbed up into his saddle, and reined his horse around. Thomas leapt from the porch and stood in front.

"Git outta the way, boy!" Ratney snarled. But Thomas skittered sideways, blocking the way.

Stephen yanked Thomas aside and grabbed the horse's bridle. "Calm down, Mr. Ratney. We can talk about—"

Ratney spurred the horse's flanks and it lunged forward, Stephen's hand still caught in the reins. He was dragged a few yards before he fell free, right beneath the horse's trampling hooves.

"*Stephen!*" Ty cried.

The horse stumbled a bit, as if about to go down. But Ratney flogged it with the reins, urging it on without looking back.

Ty, Thomas and Martha ran to Stephen. The old farmer lay still, pale as death, in the dust. Blood trickled from one corner of his mouth, staining his beard red. His right leg was twisted sideways at an impossible angle.

Thomas looked up with wide, scared eyes, and Ty's stomach wrenched.

What have I done?

FIVE

Kristi fell through darkness and dropped suddenly onto hard earth. All the air rushed from her in a great wheeze, as though an elephant had sat on her chest. She kicked and raked her fingers against the rocky dirt, but couldn't force her lungs to open. White lights flashed in her vision, like twinkling stars in a reddening sky. She planted her feet on the ground and shot her hips into the air. Her lungs finally opened and she gasped in a gulp of hot, dusty air. She turned on her side in a fit of wracking coughs.

The ground lay still beneath her, but the sickening whirling in her head kept going. As the coughing subsided, she curled into a ball and hugged her knees. Hot tears poured down her cheeks. After a minute, the spinning slowed and she lay back again, exhausted.

When she opened her eyes, she still saw only darkness. Blinking, she pressed her palms against her eyelids and rubbed. Shapes formed like shadows at night. Gradually, she made out real twinkling stars far above, then the deep purple backdrop of the sky. She turned her head and saw black, rounded ridges. After a few deep, steadying breaths, she sat up. But her head hammered sickeningly and she closed her eyes again, waiting for the pain to pass. When it did, she found she was sitting on a hard-packed dirt road. It was dusk, not yet full dark. A chirping chorus of crickets filled the air. Fireflies flashed on and off, pale green above the grass.

"Why do I *do* this to myself," she groaned, still rubbing her temples. The time machine, again just a plain, straight rod, lay beside her, its lights gone dark. She picked it up, struggled to her feet, wobbling on rubbery legs, and tried to get her bearings. A two-story farmhouse stood about a hundred yards from the road. A lantern glowed on the porch and candles flickered in the front windows. The house's sharp eaves, the big green barn to the side, all looked strangely familiar, like the faint recollection of a dream or a sudden flash of déjà vu.

"Ty!"

She winced at the new stabbing pain the yell brought, but stumbled across the uneven ground toward the house. Her legs gained strength with every step. She was sprinting by the time she reached the narrow little creek, the same one she'd washed in dozens of times. She leapt it in a single bound and raced across the yard. "Stephen! Miss Martha!"

She clomped up the wooden steps and pushed through the oak door and into Martha's kitchen. There was the long table on which she and the old woman had so often worked. Nearby, the brick oven where Kristi had burned so many loaves of bread.

"Hello? Hello! Anybody here?"

She followed the long hallway and stepped into the main house. Miss Martha, Ty, and Thomas sat hunched in chairs, each staring grimly at different walls. None of them seemed to notice her arrival.

Ty and Thomas were so different. Their tanned faces longer and thinner than she remembered. Their bodies gangly, all arms and legs.

"Hey," she called, grinning. "Did someone order a pizza from the future?"

All three faces jerked toward her. Miss Martha's eyes widened and her hand shot to her mouth. "What in providence—"

Thomas blinked. "*Kristi?*"

"Who else?" She gave a bow. "Miss me?"

Ty and Thomas jumped up and rushed at her. The three of them went down in a tangle of hugs.

"What're you doing here?" Ty gasped.

Kristi laughed. "Was in the neighborhood and thought I'd stop by to say hi."

"Let me set eyes on that girl," Martha said. Her eyes were swollen, as if she'd been crying. She reached down and pulled Kristi to her feet. "Is it really you, child?"

"Yes, it's me, Miss Martha. I missed you."

Martha threw her big arms around Kristi and squeezed. "Oh, the Lord has sent us a blessing when we needed it sorely."

Kristi closed her eyes and nuzzled into the soft, familiar bosom.

"But what're you *doing* here?" Ty asked again. "Why'd you come back? Did something happen?"

"It's a long story," Kristi said. "Where's Stephen?"

The surprise and happiness washed from each of their faces. Martha's eyes watered and she covered her mouth again.

"What?" Kristi frowned. "What's wrong?"

"He broke his leg," Ty said. "Probably has a concussion, too. He hasn't woken." He told her about the runaways and Stephen's accident.

Kristi fell back onto a hard chair. "Slaves, here? Did they get away?"

Ty shrugged. "Don't know. Ratney's horse pulled up lame after trampling Stephen. But he kept going."

"And no lame horse is going to catch Foxe after he's been given his head," Thomas added.

"But why have you come, dear?" Martha asked. "I didn't think we'd ever see you again."

Kristi took a deep breath. "I came for help." She looked at Ty and Thomas. "There was no one else I could ask. You have to help me save my uncle."

Thomas gasped. "What do you mean? You have an uncle here—in this time, I mean?"

"Not exactly." Kristi related the story of her parents' divorce, the wedding, Mimi's album and the family tree. "Jonah and Britt will be on a plantation near Chestertown, Maryland in 1858. They're going to run away, but Britt will get caught and disappear. We have to time-travel to 1858 and help them."

"*1858?*" Thomas's eyes widened. "But that's right before the Civil War. You won't be safe there, Kristi, especially in Maryland. Do you know what will happen if someone catches you?"

"I do."

Thomas shook his head. "I don't think you really understand. You can't just walk onto a plantation and take away a couple slaves. They'll arrest and whip you, maybe even hang you. Or—" he hesitated. "Or make *you* a slave, too."

Miss Martha frowned. "He's right, Kristi. Lord knows I can see why you want to help your family, but you're just a child. The risk is too great."

Kristi stiffened. "I'm *not* a child!" She took a deep breath and steadied her voice. "Britt Connors disappeared from the face of the earth just because he tried to reach freedom. He didn't hurt anyone. Or steal anything except *himself*. He didn't deserve to be punished or sold away or—or killed."

"She's right," Ty said, stepping forward. "And I'll help her."

Kristi threw her arms around his neck. "Oh, thank you, Ty. I knew it! I knew you'd help me!" She kissed his cheek.

Ty blushed and looked at the floor. "Well..."

Thomas looked incredulous. "Just like that, brother?"

"Yeah, just like that. You didn't see the boy in Philadelphia. Or the fear in Cyrus's eyes when I found him. The horror when he thought Ratney was going to take away his son. I can't stand back and just watch anymore. If I can help even one man, I'm going to do it. Bloody hanging be damned."

Thomas chuckled, even as he wrung his hands. "Then I guess I'm in, too. Hangin' be damned!"

"Wait!" Kristi held up a hand. "You can't both go."

"Why not?" they said in unison.

Kristi thought of her *twin*, Kristine, who'd been created with Thomas when Kristi and Ty had last traveled through time.

"It can only be one of you," she said. "When Kristine and I were in the time portal together, she disappeared—poof, gone forever. If you both go, the same thing might happen to you."

Ty and Thomas exchanged a wide-eyed look. Ty made a fist and held it on top of his other palm. "Rock, paper, scissors?"

Thomas sighed and shook his head. "No, you go. I know what this means to you. It means a lot to me, too, but—you should go."

"Thank you," Ty said, then stepped closer to Kristi. "So what's your scheme?"

"We go forward to 1858. Then find Thomas here on this farm."

"That's almost eighty years from now!" Thomas blurted. "I'd be, like, ninety years old." He gulped. "Or maybe not even alive anymore?"

Kristi grinned. "Oh, you'll be there. The two of you will do some amazing things, you know. You'll be just fine, Thomas. Or should I say, Dr. Jordan?"

"A bloody *doctor*?" Thomas's face screwed up in astonishment. "How in the world does *that* happen?"

Kristi opened her mouth to say more, but Thomas held up a hand. "Wait! I don't want to know."

Ty took a deep breath. "Better get moving, then."

"Stay a moment." Martha stepped between them. "It's been a horridly long day and we're all out of sorts. This is all happening too fast. You *must* first consult with Mr. Haines. I'll not have you flying off into danger while he is in this state, Ty Jordan." She turned to Kristi. "And you've only just arrived, dear. Stay here tonight. We will revisit this in the morning when we're all rested."

"There might not be time," Thomas pointed out. "What if Ratney comes back and finds Kristi here? He could cause more bloody headaches."

Ty nodded. "I'm sorry, Miss Martha. We have to go now."

Kristi took her hands. "Please understand."

"Very well." Martha's shoulders slumped. She nodded. "Godspeed, my dears. I hope you find what you're looking for."

SIX

Ty spun through a black vortex. An ear-splitting roar filled his head, pounding from the inside out, until he thought his ears must be bleeding. Then, as if a switch had been flipped, the raging wind stopped and he dropped back to earth. Gasping, he rolled to one side and dry heaved.

His stomach quieted and his head cleared, but then a chill enveloped him. Shivering, he blinked through a blur and saw he lay in a furrow of a frozen field under a gray sky. Icy air burned in his lungs. He pushed up and spotted Kristi lying a few feet away, on her back with her eyes closed. Cloudy puffs blew from her mouth and nose, like a steam engine chugging along a track.

"Kristi." He shook her shoulder. "Hey!"

Her eyes popped open and she flinched, then grimaced and cradled her head with both hands. "I'll never get used to that," she groaned, lying back rubbing up and down her bare arms. "It's so cold! It's never been cold before. What happened?"

"If we did this right, it should be February, 1858 now, remember? We left the summer sun way back in 1782."

"Then why didn't you think to bring warmer clothes?" She grumbled, sitting up and hugging herself. "You're supposed to be the brains of this operation."

"Sorry, can't think of everything. Come on, let's figure out where we are." He held out a hand and helped her to her feet.

"Is this Stephen's farm?" she asked.

The field was fallow, empty. Ty recognized the rise and fall of the earth he'd so tenderly worked and saw the familiar narrow, twisting creek in the distance. Stephen's simple house was gone. In its place sat a mammoth, sprawling Victorian farmhouse. A dozen curtained windows faced the field and two chimneys spurted gray, eddying smoke. The red barn behind it was twice as big as Stephen's had been.

"Looks like Thomas made some upgrades," Ty said, urging her toward the house. "That is, if he still lives here."

They crossed the field, jumped the frozen creek, and made their way up the steps to the porch. Ty knocked.

A moment later, a young black man pulled the door open and stepped onto the threshold. "Yes?"

"We're looking for Thomas Jordan," Ty said. "Does he live here?"

The man's forehead furrowed. He was tall and muscular with coffee-colored skin and sharp brown eyes. He stepped out, looked over Kristi and Ty's heads, then back at them. "This is Dr. Jordan's home, but he is not taking callers today."

"Tell him Ty and Kristi are here to see him," Ty said.

The man's eyes widened. "Did you say *Ty* and *Kristi*?"

Ty nodded.

The frown deepened, but the man stepped aside. "Come on in, then. Warm yourselves by the fire."

They pushed past him, through the narrow foyer, and into a room with three sofas and twice as many padded wooden chairs interspersed among tables holding colorful, hand painted vases and decorative plates on stands. A lush area rug with swirling patterns of flowers covered all but the edges of the hardwood floor. A wide window filled the outside wall, illuminating the sitting room. The opposite wall held a long bookcase with hundreds of volumes lining the shelves.

Kristi rushed to the stone fireplace against the far wall and crouched before the hearty flames, rubbing her hands.

"Name's Bo," the man said. "Dr. Jordan warned me we might someday get visitors with names such as yours."

"Is he here?" Ty asked.

Bo stared silently a moment longer, then turned and left.

"*Dr.* Jordan," Ty said when the door closed. "So you were right."

She grinned. "Good ol' Wikipedia."

"This is bloody *unreal*." Ty joined her by the fire. "What do you think he's going to look like?"

Her grin widened. "Don't know, but study hard. You're going to look the same in about eighty years."

After a few minutes, a series of thumps sounded from the other room, growing closer, accompanied by the shuffle of feet. The door burst open and a hunched old man tottered in leaning on a wooden cane. He had an unruly shock of snow-white hair and wide, bright blue eyes behind thick gold-rimmed glasses.

"Ty! Kristi! Can it really be you?"

Ty's mouth fell open. "Thomas?"

The lines and wrinkles in Thomas's face deepened as he beamed. Dropping the cane, he crossed the room like

58

a man half his age and threw his arms around them. "After all these long years," he said, sniffling. "Though not for you, I guess. You must've just left me—oh, so long ago!"

"You look, um,—good, Thomas," Kristi said.

"Don't lie now." He laughed. "I'm older than dirt and look every minute of my age." He turned to Bo, who'd trailed him back into the front room. "Put on some water for tea, would you, my boy?"

Bo picked up the cane and returned it to Thomas. "Yes sir, Dr. Jordan."

"Please sit," Thomas said, gesturing a hand wide. He grimaced as he lowered himself to a large green chair beside the fireplace. Kristi and Ty took seats on the sofa across from him.

"So, you *are* a doctor," Ty said. "Like Kristi said."

Thomas smiled. "I've dabbled in medicine, among other things, but that was a long time ago. Stephen left me the farm when he passed. We've had a successful go, I'd say."

"Oh, poor Stephen and Miss Martha," Kristi said. "What happened to them?"

"They both died peacefully in the summer of 1802. First Martha, then Stephen a few weeks later."

"So his leg mended?" Ty asked.

Thomas laughed. "There was no keeping that old bird down. He was right as rain within a few months."

"What about Cyrus and his son?" Ty asked. "I don't suppose you ever found out what happened to them?"

Thomas grinned. "Cyrus made it all the way to Buffalo before Ratney caught up with him. Cyrus broke the man's jaw, then took Xander into Canada. I know because Cyrus wrote a letter a year later, and sent payment for Foxe."

Ty smiled. "It was all worth it, then."

"It was." Thomas nodded. "Now, about your journey. I've found your family, Kristi."

She sat up straighter. "Really? Where?"

"Britt and Jonah Conwell are slaves on a plantation outside of Chestertown, Maryland, just like you said."

"No, that can't be right." Kristi frowned. "Their last name is Connors, not Conwell."

"Not yet it isn't," Thomas said. "They belong to a man named Silas Conwell, one of the biggest tobacco producers in Maryland. I've been exchanging letters with him under a false name for the last year, trying to purchase them."

"You're trying to buy my ancestors?" Kristi looked a bit affronted. "That sounds so...wrong."

"Why a false name?" Ty asked.

"The name Thomas Jordan isn't thought too highly of south of the Mason-Dixon Line. I have what you'd call a *reputation* for trouble making in the slave states, so I've been corresponding with Mr. Conwell under the guise of Horace Humphries, owner of a small tobacco plantation outside of Baltimore. An operative of mine down there has been sending and receiving the letters, but Mr. Conwell has been a bit stubborn and hasn't yet agreed to a sale."

Bo pushed the door open and entered carrying a silver tray with four steaming cups on flowery saucers. He set the tray on a table in the middle of the room and handed them each one.

"Thank you, Bo."

The young man sat in a chair with his own cup. He watched Kristi and Ty warily.

"What kind of trouble making?" Ty asked.

Thomas shrugged. "Oh, I may have helped a slave or two escape over the years."

Bo choked on his tea. "Dr. Jordan," he said. "I don't think you ought—"

"Oh, bosh." Thomas waved his warning off. "And you can call me Thomas in front of these two. They're close friends." He winked at them.

"But Dr. Jordan." Bo shook his head. "We don't know—"

"Bosh, I say," Thomas pounded his cane on the floor. "Trust them. Their hearts are as ours."

Bo let out a long breath, then crossed his arms and sat back stiffly, cup and saucer balancing on one knee. Ty watched the veins along the big man's neck bulge.

"You're working with the Underground Railroad, then," Kristi said. "I read about that, too. You've helped more than one or two escape. You're almost as big a hero as Harriet Tubman."

"Not quite." Thomas shook his head and laughed. "But, yes, this place has housed its share of wayfaring travelers."

"Is that why there are so many sofas and chairs in this room?" Ty motioned to the empty seats.

Thomas smiled. "It's been a bit slow the last few months, on account of federal marshals pushing the Fugitive Slave Law, but yes, we've been known to fill this room up."

"Bloodhound Law," Bo spat.

"What does that mean?" Kristi asked.

Thomas sighed. "That the government will go after anyone thought to be assisting runaways. Men have been arrested, some losing everything, for even feeding any black man or woman passing through. Federal marshals have been all over me, but they haven't been able to prove anything. Isn't that right, Bo?"

Bo sighed, then nodded.

"And all those marshals didn't stop Bo here from coming to me twelve years ago, in the dead of night," Thomas said.

"Really!" Kristi said. "You're an actual *runaway*? You were *on* the Underground Railroad?"

He hesitated, then nodded again. "That's correct."

"Just a ten-year-old," Thomas continued, "who'd committed the terrible crime of stealing *himself*. One of my operatives brought him here. We've *procured* documents since that say he's free. I've tried talking him into going to Canada, where it's safer, but he's almost as stubborn as you are, Kristi."

Kristi snorted and rolled her eyes.

"My place is here, Thomas," Bo said. "Helping you and others."

Ty's heart swelled with pride for his brother. He touched Thomas's arm. "I knew you'd stand up and do something. Not just sit back and let things be like...like..."

Thomas shook his head. "Don't be so hard on yourself, Ty. It took a lot of years to build this operation."

"So if Conwell won't sell Britt and Jonah, we'll go and help them escape. Take them on the underground," Kristi said. "They're going to try on their own this spring and Britt will be caught. We have to go down and get them."

"I'm afraid it's not quite that simple." Thomas sighed. "The Bloodhound Act, as Bo so aptly described it, has made it a lot more difficult to sneak slaves out of the south."

Kristi clenched her fists. "I don't care. I'll go after them."

"Don't worry. I haven't given up." Thomas petted her hand. "It's true Conwell hasn't budged, so I have a new scheme. I'll buy those boys no matter how high the cost. And they'll be free, legally."

"Great!" Kristi stood and set her tea on the table. "When do we go?"

Thomas shook his head. "You're not going to like this but—you'll not be going."

"What? Wait a minute, Thomas. You can't just keep me from—"

"Please, Kristi." Thomas held up one hand. "Hear me out. I've been thinking about this for nearly eighty years. I can't let you venture into a slave state. If something went wrong, who knows what would happen. You could disappear, just like your uncle."

"That's not *fair*!" she cried. "Nothing's going to happen to me. But even if it does, I have the time—" She stopped herself, shot a glance toward Bo, who was looking at her with raised eyebrows. She shook her head. "We've been through worse, you know that. I can take care of myself. I came all the way here to help them, not to sit around twiddling my thumbs."

Thomas sighed. "I'm not asking you to sit around, but rather to go back to where you've come from. You'll find things very different, I assure you."

"No." She crossed her arms and set her jaw. "I'm not going *anywhere* until Britt and Jonah are safe. Until they're *free*!"

Ty broke in. "What if you still can't get Conwell to sell them, Thomas? What if he says no?"

He smiled. "I have a trick or two up my sleeve. I've become a crafty old cuss. Right, Bo?"

The serious face finally broke into a thin smile. "That you are, Dr. Jordan. A crafty ol' cuss, for sure."

SEVEN

Kristi lifted the hem of her skirt and stepped from Thomas's covered carriage onto the gravel walkway before the train station. Thomas had outfitted her with period clothing, from the stores he kept on-hand for the steady stream of runaways coming through his farm. Of course she'd complained about having to leave her jeans and polo behind to a don puffy dress, but as the icy wind enveloped her, carrying with it the acrid stink of burning coal from the waiting train, she was happy to have the woolen cape to wrap more tightly around herself.

A long train of passenger, box, and steerage cars curved around the station's platform and extended another hundred yards along the tracks behind. At its head stood a black engine with a giant smokestack issuing puffs of grayish smoke and a grill-like cattle guard jutting from the front, giving it a dark, menacing look.

She reached up to assist Thomas from the carriage. His bony hand was cold, the skin loose, like a raw chicken out of the fridge. He held the rail with his other hand and eased down the two metal steps and crunched onto the gravel.

"Thank you, my girl." He let go of her hand and braced the small of his back. "Afraid this old body isn't much good for long carriage rides anymore."

"Welcome," she said stiffly.

He opened his mouth, as if to say something else, but she turned and tromped a few steps away. She didn't want to hear any more apologies for leaving her behind. There wasn't anything he could say to make her feel better.

Ty stepped off next, then Bo, carrying two carpetbags and a leather satchel.

Thomas turned to his driver, an older black man with a thin, wrinkled face and graying mustache. "Get these two young folks home safely, Robert. And don't fall for any of Kristi's shenanigans. She's a sly one." He winked at her. She rolled her eyes and turned her back to him.

"Take care of him, Bo," Ty said, shaking the big man's hand. He turned to Thomas. "Good luck, brother."

"Don't need luck when you're doing what's right," Thomas said. "We'll be home within the week with our two new friends. Have no fear, Kristi."

"Hmph." Kristi climbed up back into the carriage.

Thomas sighed, then ambled toward the platform, Bo at his side holding one elbow.

Ty stepped back up into the carriage and sat across from Kristi. "Now what?"

She shrugged one shoulder and looked out the window. Bo and Thomas had boarded the train. As the carriage lurched forward, Kristi stood, braced her hands on either side of the doorframe, and leaned out. The driver was hidden from her view. She turned and grinned at Ty.

He shook his head. "Don't even *think* of it, Kristi!"

"I'm not *thinking* about anything." She gathered the long skirt up, then leapt from the carriage and ran to an alley between two shuttered warehouses.

Ty was at her side a moment later, panting. "What the heck are you *doing*?"

"What do you think? Thomas thinks he's just going to leave us behind while he goes after *my* family." She poked her head out of the alley as the carriage turned a corner and disappeared. "Well, forget that. Come on."

With her skirt bunched in one hand, she took off toward the train, ignoring Ty's shouts for her to stop. A sharp, high whistle tore the air. White steam erupted from the sides of the engine and the stack belched a thick gray cloud. The train lurched, then eased forward at a crawl.

Avoiding the passenger cars, Kristi ran along the box cars, spotted a ladder hanging off the side of one, and leapt for it. She grasped the cold metal rungs with both hands and kicked her skirt out of the way to get both feet firmly on the bottom rung. Then she turned and held out a hand for Ty.

"Come on!"

The train was picking up speed as Ty sprinted along beside it, reaching for her hand. Holding the thin rung with only fingertips, she stretched until she grazed Ty's fingertips, but she couldn't get a hold and he fell back a few feet again.

"Hurry!" she screamed.

He lowered his head, pushed harder, and lunged. This time she grasped his hand and swung him toward the ladder. They crashed together and one of her feet caught in her skirt. Just as her fingers slipped, Ty grabbed hold of her waist, steadying her.

"You all right?" he yelled over the sound of the wind and grinding wheels.

"No! I *hate* wearing skirts."

Ty grinned. "Yeah, me too. Ladies first?" He gestured up the ladder.

"I *don't* think so."

He laughed and climbed the ladder and she followed.

* * *

Hours later, Ty had to clench his teeth to keep them from chattering. He and Kristi had huddled shivering together on top of the boxcar, exposed to the frigid wind, as the train passed hundreds of homesteads, through a forest of evergreens, and over a few rivers. He stuffed frozen, numb fingers into his armpits. His eyelids grew heavy and he caught himself dozing for brief moments, only to jerk back awake at the feeling of falling.

"I c-can't stay up here anymore," Kristi croaked. "I can't even f-feel my f-face."

"All right, let's find a car to get into." He unwrapped his arms and struggled to hands and knees, feeling as though he were trying to move through syrup. He led the way across the top of the car. A two-foot gap separated the car from the next, another boxcar. He stretched his arms and crossed over, then looked back to make sure Kristi crossed the chasm safely as well.

After crawling across four more boxcars, Ty found the first passenger car. "Wait here," he said.

He swung a leg over the side and had to put his arm through the rung of the ladder and hold with the crook of his elbow because he didn't trust his frozen hands to hold him. Halfway down the ladder, he looked through the small window in the door and found dozens of black men and women packed together in the car, some in chains. He quickly ascended the ladder again.

"Gotta keep moving. It's a slave car."

Kristi shook her head. "I don't care. My hands are going to fall off if I don't get warm soon."

"You'll care if they think you're a slave. Come on."

They crossed that car and two others before Kristi grabbed his leg.

"I—I can't go anymore."

He nodded and swung a leg over the edge again and helped Kristi get purchase with her trembling hands on the ladder as well. He eased himself onto the coupler between the cars and helped Kristi down.

She seemed to force a quivering smile. "Any chance of s-some hot ch-chocolate in this next c-car?"

Ty smiled. "I'll see what I can—"

The door of the car behind them slid open and a hand jutted out to grab Ty's shoulder.

"Not so fast, boy!"

* * *

Kristi's legs burned as a pale man with rough, unshaven cheeks and chin and pinched, beady eyes ushered her through the train car with a vise-grip on her arm. The car was filled with other black people, but the men wore trousers and the women skirts, so she guessed it to be a car of free-blacks, not slaves. Just as she realized this, she spotted Bo toward the front of the car. His eyes widened.

She opened her mouth to call to him for help, but he glared, as if screaming with his eyes to keep her mouth shut. She did, then glanced back at Ty, who was being dragged by the man as she was being shoved.

At the end of the car, the man let go of her arm to open the door. It was then that she saw the pistol tucked into his belt, inches from her hand. She could get

68

it, maybe fire a couple shots into the ceiling and escaped with Ty in the confusion, just like in countless movies she'd seen.

"Don't even think about it!" the man growled, as if reading her mind. He snatched her arm again and shoved her and Ty against the wall in the next car, which was empty, but for one man. "Look'ee what I got here, Mackey."

The new man was lanky with a long, hooked nose, leathery face and greasy black hair pulled into ponytail. He wore a ruffled white shirt beneath a faded blue vest and tan riding trousers with a bit of fray at the ends above grayish stockings. A cowhide whip hung from his belt. "Do tell, Matthews."

"Couple o' stow'ways crawling on top of the train and sneakin' into the darkies' car. Mayhap another runaway and reward."

The man named Mackey approached, eyes narrowed and smiling in a slimy way that made Kristi's skin crawl.

"Where you run away from, girl?"

"Let me go!" Kristi spat. "I'm not a runaway!"

Mackey's smile widened. He tapped the handle of the whip with dirty fingers. "Got you a sharp tongue, too. Mayhap you need learning on how to speak to a white man."

"Please sir," Ty began. "You don't underst—"

"Shut up, you!" Matthews kicked him in the back of his legs, forcing him to his knees.

Mackey grabbed a hold of the back of Kristi's neck.

"Got a price on yer hide?"

She spat in his face.

"You little hellcat!" Mackey ripped the whip from his belt. Four strands, knots tied on the ends, hung from the handle. "Yer gonna pay for that!"

A dark blur rushed into the car, knocking Matthews to the floor. Before Mackey had time to react, Bo stood up straight, brandishing the other man's pistol.

"Let 'em go!"

Mackey spun, wrapping his arm around Kristi's neck and keeping her between him and Bo. "This ain't your concern, boy. Git on outta here 'fore you get yo'self a whippin' too."

Bo aimed the pistol at Mackey's head. "I said *let her go*, mister."

Mackey looked at him, then at Matthews, who had regained his feet and stood seething, fists clenched. "There's two of us, boy, and only one of you."

Bo pulled back the hammer of the pistol. "Yeah? In five seconds, it'll just be him and me."

Mackey's jaw tightened. "You'll be lynched for aimin' that gun at a white man, boy."

"Then you and me'll dance with the devil together," Bo said coolly. "Two seconds."

Mackey swore and let go of Kristi's neck. She coughed and moved with Ty behind Bo. The train gave a long whistle and jerked as it slowed, throwing her off-balance. Bo steadied his stance, keeping the pistol on Mackey.

"Now what, boy?" Mackey snarled. "You ain't got nowhere to run."

"Get on outta here." Bo motioned to the door.

"This ain't over!" Mackey growled. "I'm gonna hunt you down like the coon that you are."

Bo nodded. "I'm lookin' forward to it."

Still glaring, the two men backed from the car. Bo slammed the door on them, ripped a bar from the overhead rack, and used it to jam the door shut.

"Thanks!" Kristi said, rubbing her sore neck.

"No time for thanks." He stowed the gun under his coat and ushered them through the next two cars, stopping them in the open air before the next. The cold wind blew through Kristi's skirt.

Bo turned to Ty. "Go find Thomas and tell him to meet us at Ford's tavern. He knows it."

"*Meet* you? What are you talking about?"

"She just spit on a white man and I aimed a gun at him. You heard him. He ain't gonna let that go."

Kristi raised her hands. "But, how—"

"I said there's no time! Ford's Tavern. You got that, boy?"

Ty frowned and looked at Kristi.

She sighed. "Go get Thomas."

Ty nodded and ran through the next car.

"So what are *we* going to do?" Kristi asked.

"We gotta jump."

"*Jump?*" She looked down at the ground moving swiftly past. "Are you crazy?"

"Make sure you clear the train. Roll when you hit the ground and stay down until the train has passed."

Kristi's breath caught in her throat as she looked down again. She'd felt the train slowing, but those trees just beyond the tracks still seemed to whip past. "But—"

"If those men find a sheriff or constable, we're in a lot of trouble. We gotta get off this train before it gets to the station."

She bit her lip. *This is gonna hurt!* She braced her hands on either car, took a deep breath, then leapt. She cleared the train easily, landing in a ditch two feet beyond the tracks. The momentum swept her feet from under her and she tumbled, jarring one shoulder and skinning both knees and elbows. A moment later Bo was down, too, landing twenty yards beyond. She stayed down, the scrapes and scratches burning like fire, and watched the train pass by.

EIGHT

T y raced through the cars toward the front of the train, checking each cabin for Thomas. In one, he'd seen a white haired man through the window and burst in. But the gentleman was thirty years too young and the intrusion won Ty the shriek of the gentleman's wife and a handbag to the side of the head that had left him woozy.

In the next car, a teenaged boy with rich, mahogany skin and a maroon cap and coat buttoned to the throat stopped him. "Suh, you'll have to return to your car. We'll be debarking soon."

"I'm looking for Thomas Jordan," Ty said. "It's an emergency."

"Sorry, suh. Don't know who that is."

"An old man with a cane."

The porter shrugged. "Lot's o' old men with canes on this train, suh."

"I mean *really* old, like ninety."

The porter's face screwed up. He nodded after a couple seconds. "There's a really old fella in cabin thirty-four, I think."

"Which way?"

"Next car up."

"Thanks!" Ty rushed past and into the next car. He counted the cabins down from forty. There, in thirty-four, Thomas sat with eyes closed, head leaning against the window and his cane clutched to his chest. A middle-aged man in a brown suit sat next to him and two other gentlemen in black suits sat across.

Ty burst in and fell on Thomas, shaking his shoulders. "Thomas, wake up."

Thomas's eyes snapped open. He looked around quizzically and blinked a few times, as if unsure of what he was seeing. "Ty? What in God's name are you—"

"No time!" He looked at the surprised faces of the others in the car. "I'm sorry for the intrusion," he said. "It's an emergency."

"Ty Jordan!" Thomas slammed the butt of his cane against the floor. "*What* are you *doing* here? Where's Kristi?"

Ty took a deep breath. "She's gone!"

* * *

Ty and Thomas pushed off the train and onto the wooden platform of the station. Ty shielded his eyes from the bright afternoon sun and scanned the debarking passengers for Mackey and Matthews, but caught no sight of them.

"Come on," Thomas growled, the first two words he'd spoken, apart from occasional curses, since Ty'd relayed the events to him.

Thomas led the way through the station house and onto the street. Ty followed behind with the carpetbags and satchel.

The street was busy with carriages and wagons. A hotel stood on the other side with a tavern and stables on either side of it.

A covered Landau carriage hitched to two brown mares stood just up the street. A tall man Ty guessed to be in his early twenties stood by the horses, adjusting the straps. His black skin stood out against his clean white shirt and stiff tan breeches.

"Pardon me," Thomas said. "Do you know Ford's Tavern?"

"Sure do, suh."

Thomas nodded and tossed a coin. "Then get us there quickly."

The boy caught it, grinned, and opened the door. "Yessuh. Where'er you say. Name's George." He took the carpetbags from Ty, but Thomas grabbed the satchel and held on.

Ty helped Thomas climb onto the folding step and inside. Just before he stepped in himself, he looked down the street. There, thirty yards away, Matthews sat astride a white mare. Mackey stood a bit farther down the street. On his left a slumped a black man in a dirty, threadbare shirt, a rope wrapped around his neck. Mackey held the other end. He looked Ty's way and Ty lunged into the carriage and slammed the door.

Twenty minutes later, just outside of the town proper, Thomas signaled to the driver to pull the carriage over. "Stand outside and look for them," he instructed Ty.

Ty looked through the window. They were stopped at the edge of a wood of cedars. A small structure stood a hundred yards farther down the road, smoke curling from its chimney. Three or four horses were tied to the posts in front. "Won't they be at the tavern?"

"They're not *allowed* at the tavern. Now get outside where they can see you."

Ty left the carriage without further protest, wrapping his coat around himself and stuffing his hands into the pockets.

"Why are we stoppin' here, suh?" the driver called down.

"We're—uh—waiting for someone."

The driver shrugged. "Wha'ever you say, suh."

After twenty minutes, two figures appeared in the shadows of the trees. Ty raised a hand and waved. A few seconds later, Bo and Kristi emerged through the bushes. Kristi limped slightly. Her dress was torn down the side and covered with dirt.

"What happened to you?" He reached out and picked some grass from her hair.

"Had to jump off the train."

"How was that?"

"Awesome, Ty." She rolled her eyes. "Just awesome."

"Get in here quickly," Thomas called from the carriage. Ty noticed Kristi avoiding Thomas's eyes as she climbed in. The old man turned to the driver. "Can you take us to an inn that will allow my servants, George?"

"I know jus' the place. They'll have to sleep in the stables, though."

Thomas nodded. "That'll do." He turned back and sat next to Bo on the bench seat, across from Kristi and Ty, as the carriage jolted on down the road.

He took a deep breath. "Are you all right, Kristi? Those men on the train didn't hurt you, did they?"

"I'm okay, thanks." She looked up at him and smiled, looking relieved that he didn't yell at her. "Banged my knee a little jumping off the train, but it's fine. Thomas, I'm sorry I—"

"Maddness!" Thomas jammed his cane onto the floor so hard Ty wondered why it didn't break through. His face instantaneously transformed from concerned to hopping mad. "Ill-conceived, irresponsible, *madness!*" he roared, glaring back and forth between them.

Kristi slunk back, looking cowed for the moment. Ty did the same.

"Do you have any idea how much trouble you were in? How much trouble you're *still* in? This is no game! Do you know what those men were?"

Kristi shook her head, gaze fixed on the floor. Bo sat arrow straight with arms crossed, face stoic.

"Slave catchers, that's what. Their *job* is to sniff out runaways, to drag them back to their plantations. If Bo hadn't been there, who knows what would have happened to you."

"I'm sorry," Kristi said again. "Don't be mad at Ty. It's my fault. I just wanted to be part of this, to help Jonah and Britt. I didn't think—"

"No. You *didn't* think! That's the problem! You ignored my instructions and jumped into the fire with both feet." He closed his eyes and sighed, rubbing his temples. When he looked up a moment later, the fire in his eyes was gone, spent as quickly as it had ignited. His wrinkled face was pale, except for the dark circles around his swollen, tired eyes. He ran one hand through his thin hair. "This is just unbelievable."

"Really, Thomas?" Kristi said, shrugging. "I mean— you know us. Did you *really* think we'd just go quietly back to the farm and wait?"

Thomas chuckled at that. "No, I should've known. This old head must be slipping."

"So now what?" Ty said. "We're here. How can we help?"

Thomas shook his head. "No, I won't hear of it. Kristi and Bo have already made enemies of slave catchers who can cause us a good bit of trouble. No, tomorrow we'll have to figure out how to get you two back to Pennsylvania."

"If that man Mackey reports to the constable, they'll be watching the railroad, Thomas," Bo said. "We're gonna have trouble getting back north from here."

Thomas sighed. "You've really buggered this whole scheme, young lady."

Kristi nodded and looked down again.

"So, we can't turn back," he continued. "The only thing now is for you two to take that time machine right out of here. Go home, leave the job to me and Bo."

Ty looked up in surprise at the mention of the time machine. Kristi's eyes widened, too. They looked toward Bo, but his stoic expression hadn't changed.

"Oh, don't worry about him." Thomas waved a hand. "I've already told him all about it. He thinks I'm off my rocker, though. Isn't that right, Bo?"

The other man raised his eyebrows, as if to say *'Whatever you say, you crazy old codger'*, but didn't answer.

Kristi stomped one foot. "I'm *not* going back without Britt and Jonah."

Thomas sighed. "No, I suppose not. Next thing I know you'd be flashing right onto that plantation and into captivity. All right, the two of you had better come along. But you *must* do as I say, no matter what. You do *not* leave Bo's or my side, you hear?"

"Yes, sir," Kristi and Ty said in unison.

"Good, then my first order is to remain quiet while an old man takes a nap."

* * *

An hour later, as the sun set over the trees, the carriage pulled up before a wide stone building with a gray slate roof. Candles burned in tall sash windows on either side of a brown, wooden door.

Thomas flipped the driver another coin, then turned to Bo. "I'll make the arrangements." He looked down at Ty. "Come on in with me."

Kristi sat on a wooden crate against the outside wall of the inn, arms wrapped about herself to stave off the cold. She heard a whinny and looked up the road. A lone rider was turning his horse to head away from the inn. In the failing light, she couldn't make out who it was, but the horse's haunches were snow-white.

"Bo," she called, jumping up and pointing. "Who's that?"

He frowned as he gazed in that direction. The rider disappeared around a bend. Bo grunted and ran a hand over the handle of the gun still tucked into his belt.

A few minutes later Thomas and Ty came out of the inn. Ty handed Kristi a loaf of bread and two cold, mushy potatoes.

"I'm sorry about all this," he said, not looking up to meet her eyes.

"Remember that I am Horace Humphries," Thomas said. "From a tobacco plantation outside of Baltimore. The two of you are my servants."

"You mean *slaves*." The word tasted like vinegar in Kristi's mouth. "We have to pretend to be slaves."

Thomas nodded.

"Whatever."

"And the two of you will have to sleep out in the stables," Thomas added.

"I've bedded in worse, Mr. Humphries," Bo said.

Kristi rolled her eyes. "I guess I have, too, at summer camp. What's the plan for tomorrow?"

"Conwell's plantation lies outside of Chestertown, a couple hours by carriage. We'll call on him in the morning and see what we can do about Jonah and Britt."

"But what if he says no?" Kristi asked. "Maybe he still won't let them go."

Thomas motioned toward the satchel hanging from Bo's shoulder. "Don't worry, m' girl. A heavy purse can soften the hardest heart. We won't be leaving without them."

He handed a lantern to Bo, who gave the carpetbags to Ty and the leather satchel to Thomas. "This will be safer with you, I think."

Thomas nodded. He and Ty said their good-nights and went back into the inn. Kristi and Bo circled around the back. There a long, wooden shed with large, barn half-doors stood. The black iron hinges creaked when Bo pulled them open. It smelled earthy, a mixture of dirt, straw, and manure. Drafts blew through gaps in the walls. Two horses stretched their necks over stall doors to view the newcomers, then disappeared back into the stalls.

Kristi wrapped her arms around herself again. "On second thought, maybe I haven't slept in worse."

Bo grunted and led her on down the middle aisle. The next two stalls were occupied not by horses but by black men. Bo nodded over the half-doors as they passed. They lifted their heads to return the greeting, but didn't say anything.

"In here." Bo opened the next door, a small compartment with a layer of straw covering the floor. "I'll be in that next stall." He handed her his knife.

She gaped at it. "What's this for?"

"Keep that blade close, girl," he said, loud enough for both horse and men to hear.

"Oh. Uh—right." She nodded. "Good night."

Bo shut both halves of the Dutch door. She heard him enter the next stall, the rustle of straw, and finally a tired groan. Then, silence.

Kristi kicked the straw into a pile against the wall and lay down. The prickly stuff poked and scratched and the dust made her sneeze. But it was softer than bare ground. Her mouth tasted sour and she found herself missing, of all things, toothpaste and a toothbrush.

Clutching the knife to her chest, she closed her eyes, but her mind spun too fast to allow sleep in. She pictured Jonah and Britt running from baying dogs through swamps and across rivers. She thought about Britt getting caught. What will happen to him? If he isn't taken back to his plantation, where will he end up?

She thought about the other two men sleeping in the stables. Were they slaves or free men? If they belonged to the innkeeper, would they try to run away someday? A pang of guilt twisted her stomach. She'd complained about spending just one night here. How many did those men spend sleeping like livestock? Had either ever slept in a real bed?

It wasn't fair. She yawned deeply, wishing she could stay in 1858 long enough to help ALL the slaves in Maryland escape. But of course that wasn't possible for one person, even Harriet Tubman.

Just as sleep started its slow creep up her limbs, a hinge creaked in the dark. She shot up and held the knife out with both hands. But her stall was empty, the doors still closed. She heard shuffling in the space next to hers, where one of the slaves had lain. Then muffled whispers. Holding her breath, she eased closer and pressed an ear to the wall.

"You hear talk o' Moses?" whispered a hoarse voice.

"I heared talk," another answered.

"Moses come back ta Mar'lan'."

Moses? Kristi thought. *What are they talking about?*

"Dere's some unda'groun' folks around."

Underground? Then it hit her. Of course. *Harriet Tubman—The Moses of her people.* They were talking about Tubman!

One of the men clicked his tongue. "Jus' you show me da way ta dat unda'groun'."

"Dey say it lead to Canaan."

"I don' care iffn it takes me ta Jericho, long as it rides me outta this hell-hole."

Kristi crept back to her straw mattress and stared up at the rafters. Harriet Tubman was right here in Maryland, helping slaves escape. What if they ran into her? What if they could help her? Kristi could help make history by saving more slaves than just Jonah and Britt. *Kristi Connors, conductor on the Underground Railroad.* She smiled to herself and finally relaxed enough to let sleep come in.

* * *

The cold, bumpy carriage ride to Conwell's plantation rattled Kristi's bones, making her already aching head pound harder. She sat next to Ty on the hard bench, grumpy from the long, cold night in the straw. She turned her head in wide circles, still trying to work a kink out of her neck as they crossed the Maryland countryside.

Thomas and Bo sat across. Bo held the leather satchel on his lap. They'd risen at dawn, eaten a cold breakfast of hard biscuits and over-salted bacon, and set off in the frigid morning air. But now, after nearly two hours in a jolting carriage, the sun was shining bright and warm for a February morning. They'd passed dozens of farms and small communities. Most of the fields were fallow, just empty frozen brown clumps.

"You're sure they said *Moses*," Thomas asked for the tenth time. "You're sure they weren't just talking about the Bible, or—"

"I told you that's what I heard," she muttered. "But they never said Harriet Tubman's name. Just that Moses had come back to Maryland, on the underground, taking slaves to a place called Cana, or something like that."

"You mean Canaan," Bo corrected.

"Yeah, that's it. Where is that? Canada?"

"For some, it is." Thomas smiled. "It's from the Bible. Canaan was the Promised Land for the Israelites, the place where God meant them to be free. Now it's code for the slaves and the Underground Railroad. It means freedom from the shackles of slavery, wherever that can be found."

"Their own Promised Land," Kristi said.

"Thousands of slaves set off for Canaan," Thomas said. "But only a few of the lucky ones will make it. Others, like your uncle, won't. That's why we're here."

"Isn't there more we can do?" Kristi asked. "I mean, helping my family is one thing, but what about all those other slaves, just in Maryland alone? When we're done, shouldn't we find Harriet Tubman and help her."

"Oh, Ms. Tubman will do just fine without us calling attention to her work," Thomas said. "That's why they call her Moses. She'll guide hundreds of runaways to their own Canaan. It's been my life's work to help them once they've arrived."

"What do you mean?" Ty asked.

"You can't take a man out of the fields and expect him to suddenly have all the skills needed to prosper and provide for his family. It has been illegal for these people to learn to read and write. Their only identity has been the limited one allowed by their masters. Without help, their Canaan will turn from a Promised Land into a world of poverty and starvation. A whole different form of slavery."

"So how do *you* help them?" Kristi asked.

Thomas puffed his thin chest. "I *educate* them."

"Really?" She wrinkled her nose. "Is that all?"

Thomas laughed. "It may not sound as glamorous as secret passages and harrowing escapes from bloodhounds, but education is the most lasting path to independence. I take runaways in and teach them to read and write, to do their numbers. Give them land, sometimes, and teach them to cultivate it, to shoe horses, to smith iron. I help them support themselves, and in turn, they help others. Like our friend here."

Bo nodded.

Kristi sat back and looked out the window of the carriage. She'd heard this lecture before, but from her father, who always accused her of skating by in school. Getting B's and C's when she should've pulled A's, as if grades were the most important thing in the world. He always went on and on about how education and hard work had carried him out of poverty. And she always rolled her eyes.

The carriage swayed to make a wide turn. The wheels crunched on crushed shells that covered a long drive. Kristi stood, gripped both sides of the doorframe, and stuck her head out. Leafless trees lined the long drive, which led to a row of structures. Concrete steps at the end of the drive led to the Big House, a wide, boxy, two-story brick manor with eight windows with blue shutters across the faces of two wings with an arched doorway between. Attached to the left of the Big House was a single story kitchen house with smoke curling from the chimney. To the right, separated from the others, were three more structures, none much bigger than sheds. Their walls were unpainted, gray boards with mud plastered between slats, roofs warped cedar shingles.

Kristi shuddered.

The carriage stopped before a wide stone patio. A black man in a dark suit and regal air ambled from the kitchen door and down the stairs. He was tall, but a bit hunched in the shoulders, looking to be about her dad's age, but moving with the halting gait of a much older man. He opened the carriage door and bowed to Thomas.

"Afternoon, suh," he murmured. "Welcome to Woodland Manor."

Thomas stepped from the carriage with Bo's assistance. "My name is Mr. Horace Humphries. I have business with the master of this plantation, Mr. Conwell."

The man glanced back at the front door and shook his head. "Is Massa Conwell spectin' you, Mista Humphries? He don' normally take callers afore noontime."

Thomas's forehead wrinkled. "No."

"I'm sorry, suh. But, Massa don' take call—"

"What's your name, son?" Thomas asked.

"Gerald, suh."

"Gerald, my companions and I have traveled a long way to meet with Mr. Conwell. This old body is too racked with rheumatism to leave and call again. I understand your master is an important, busy man. But may I request that you announce my call when prudence dictates?"

Gerald shifted his feet and looked warily back at the door for a few seconds, then nodded.

"You ken come wait a spell in the parlor, but I can't announce you even a minute afore noontime." He looked at Kristi and Bo. "Your people ken wait in da kitchen."

"That will be fine," Thomas said.

The sound of quick moving, clomping hooves carried on the wind. Kristi turned to see riders coming quickly up the drive.

Her throat went dry. There were three of them, two white men with a black man between them. Blood was splattered across the front of the black man's tattered gray shirt. His wrists were cinched to the saddle horn. A rope hung around his neck. Holding the other end of the rope was an unshaven man with a hooked nose and hair pulled back into a ponytail.

"Oh, no!" Kristi croaked. "*Mackey!*"

NINE

Well, I'll be." Mackey deftly swung off his horse and pulled a pistol from the saddlebag. His companion climbed down with less grace and withdrew his own gun. Mackey approached them, the tip of his tongue darting in and out of his mouth like a serpent tasting the air for prey. "Lookee what the cat drug in, Matthews." He raised the gun.

Bo stepped in front of Kristi and Ty.

"Step back!" Thomas barked at him. He turned and glared at the approaching man. "Lower your weapon, sir!"

"I ain't lowerin' nothin', old man!" He aimed the gun over Thomas's shoulder.

"*Peace*, sir!" Thomas pushed the hand with the gun up. "This man belongs to *me*!"

"Git your hands off me!" Mackey shoved Thomas's shoulder. "Ain't gonna be no peace 'til that boy's strung up!"

Bo bent, readying to jump the man.

"Stay your weapon, Mr. McNamara," called a voice from behind them. Ty spun to see a tall man in a gray suit, vest, and long waistcoat that hung to his knees. His black hair was salted and thick, lamb chop sideburns framed a handsome face.

Mackey threw his hands in the air. "This boy aimed a gun at me, Mr. Conwell."

"Like the gentleman said, Mr. McNamara, it is *his* man. Do you have the money to compensate him if you harm his Negro?"

"No, but—"

"Welcome home, Jethro," Conwell said over him, turning to the slave still tied to his mount. "I trust you didn't give Mr. McNamara and Mr. Matthews much trouble bringing you home."

"No, suh." He was as wide as a Rugby player, but his shoulders slumped forward and his head hung low. One of his eyes was swollen shut and a deep gash split his bottom lip.

"Mr. Matthews, take Jethro to his quarters. I'll deal with him in due time."

Matthews nodded, stuffed his pistol back into the waist of his pants, and led the horse carrying the man away.

"And what business have you here, sir?" Conwell said, turning back to Thomas.

"My name's Horace Humphries, Mr. Conwell." He bowed formally. "We've been corresponding for some time about a business proposal."

Conwell seemed to study him a moment, then nodded. "Yes, I recall, Mr. Humphries. You wish to purchase two of my Negros for breeding stock."

"I do, sir."

"I also recall rebuffing your proposition, Mr. Humphries. And yet, you've come anyway."

"I do hope you'll forgive my calling in person, but I thought it prudent to meet with you face to face to offer a price more to your liking."

Conwell looked at him a moment longer before nodding. "This is not the place to discuss such business. Gerald?"

The butler stepped up. "Yessuh?"

"Take our guests around back to the porch and bring tea."

Gerald nodded. "Yessuh."

"Mr. McNamara, if you would join me in the house."

Mackey glared at Bo a moment longer, then followed Conwell into the house, grumbling.

"Right this way, Mista Humphries," Gerald motioned.

They followed the butler around the house. A long, sloped yard led to a creek winding through the fields in the distance. The covered back porch was paved with stone and as wide as the Big House. A swing hung anchored to the beam on the far end and a round, iron table, six feet across, sat under the covering.

"You ken wait here, suh," Gerald said, then disappeared into the kitchen.

"What's happening, Thomas?" Kristi whispered.

"We're going to do some business. You and Bo stand behind us, at least five feet, and look at the ground, not a Conwell. Say *nothing*. Regardless of what you hear, say *nothing*, hear?"

She nodded and stepped back.

Conwell and Mackey emerged from the house a few minutes later. Conwell sat, motioning for Thomas to do the same. Ty stood at Thomas's shoulder, holding his cane. Mackey stood to Conwell's right, the angry glare gone. He glanced at Bo and smirked, as if knowing a nasty secret. Ty fought the urge to look back at Bo and hoped the man was looking at the ground as Thomas had directed and hadn't seen the evil smile.

Gerald returned a minute later with a tray with two cups and saucers, a white teakettle with blue flowers painted around the base, and a small wooden box. He set saucers and cups in front of Conwell and Thomas, poured tea into both, then extended the box to Conwell, who withdrew a fat cigar. Gerald lit the cigar with a match.

"Care for a cigar, Mr. Humphries?" he asked, sitting back with a great cloud of smoke enveloping his head. "Rolled with the finest tobacco grown right here on this plantation. You're a tobacco man yourself, are you not, Mr. Humphries? You'll no doubt appreciate the quality."

"Don't mind if I do." Thomas took a cigar and Gerald lit it. "But mine is but a small farm, Mr. Conwell. Nothing like your operation, nor do we produce near the quality of this fine tobacco."

Conwell smiled and took another puff. "If you have but a small farm, Mr. Humphries, what need have you for more Negros?"

"I wish to leave my grandson the means to grow the farm." He nodded toward Ty. "My Negro is as strong as an ox, but lazy and not bright enough to work a farm without an overseer. But if you'd sell me two hard working boys with experience planting and the seed to provide my grandson with whelps, he'll be set up to grow."

Conwell puffed away, considering. Then he nodded. "I have two boys who fit the description. Brothers, I believe."

"And what is your asking price?"

Conwell sighed. "This is where we run into a problem, Mr. Humphries, as I stated in my letters. For I have but two young bucks and they are two of my finest, both strong as oxen and virile as Hercules himself."

Thomas folded his hands. "And what price would you put on such Herculean boys?"

Conwell put a hand on his chest. "Can you put a price on the heart? For I have raised those boys from pups." The man was smiling, but if he'd been a cartoon character, Ty imagined dollar signs would have replaced his shining pupils.

"I'm sure we can come to an accord, Mr. Conwell. I am prepared to give you $400."

Conwell laughed, leaning back and putting his hands on his knees. "$400 is but a drop in the bucket to the worth and esteem with which I hold those two boys. Four hundred dollars, *each*, to begin." Conwell narrowed his eyes. "But, to finalize the deal, I'll require your man, there." He motioned to Bo. "Eight hundred dollars won't fill the void left on my farm. I'll need your man's strong arms just to begin to recoup my losses."

Ty struggled to keep his jaw from dropping. He ached to look back at Bo.

But Thomas merely smiled. "I've already said my man is dull and lazy. What need would you have of him?"

Conwell shrugged. "I don't need brains, Mr. Humphries, just brawn. And the crack of a whip is enough the cure any Negro of laziness." He took another puff. "That is my offer, Mr. Humphries. If you are not interested, then this engagement has run its course, for I have much work pressing."

Thomas's face reddened and the smile fell from his lips. As if seeing his advantage, Conwell smirked and leaned forward. "What shall it be, Mr. Humphries? You wish to grow your farm and I can provide the means."

Thomas tapped his cigar on the side of the table, then sighed. "May I examine the boys?"

This time, Ty's jaw did drop. What was Thomas playing at? He couldn't possibly be considering Conwell's proposal. He snuck a look back at Bo and

Kristi. They both stood, stiff as boards, looking at the ground.

"Of course. Gerald, fetch the brothers."

Ty leaned down to Thomas's ear. "What are you doing?" he hissed.

Thomas waved him away as he would a mosquito buzzing by his ear.

A few minutes later, Gerald returned, leading two boys. The first was tall, muscular, his hair cropped close. He was a few years older than Kristi, his skin a few shades darker. His head was up, dark eyes staring straight ahead, but not at any of them. His lips were pressed tight, expression stoic, unaffected. The other was younger, perhaps eight or nine, with thin, scrawny arms. His gaze never left the stone in front of his feet.

Thomas stood and examined the boys, pinching their arms as Ty had seen the slaver in Philadelphia do. It made his skin crawl.

"What are your names?" Thomas asked.

"Jonah, suh," the bigger one said without looking up. "That's my brother, Britt."

Ty snuck another look back, this time at Kristi. She wasn't looking down anymore, but up at the boys with wide eyes.

Thomas nodded. "I'll give you six-hundred."

"Seven-hundred," Conwell countered. "Not a penny less."

Thomas's head bobbed, as if he were doing calculations. "Very well. Seven hundred dollars."

"And your Negro?" Conwell said.

Thomas sighed, not looking at Ty, Bo, or Kristi. "*And my Negro.*"

* * *

"He can't do this!" Kristi yelled, grabbing Bo's arm. She and Bo had been relegated to the kitchen while the *masters* finalized the deal.

Bo knelt and wiped a tear from her cheek. "We trade one soul for two and come out ahead."

"But it's not right!" she blurted, knocking his hand away. "How can he just sell you? You're not even a slave!"

"I've done it before and I can do it again." He lowered his voice. "Besides, if they'd have negotiated much longer, Conwell could have asked for you as well."

"It's not fair!" she sobbed.

"Life ain't fair," Bo said. "You take those two boys out of here and set them up real nice, real safe, and don't you worry about me." He winked. "Thomas has a plan."

"Plan? What plan?"

"Hush now," he said. "And let things play out as they must."

Gerald fetched them twenty minutes later.

When Kristi stepped back outside, cold, gray clouds had filled the sky, blotting out what had been a bright, sunny morning. Icy wind rattled the finger-like branches of the oak beside Conwell's house and worked its way through her dress and coat, sending goose bumps up her arms and down her body.

But the cold couldn't compare to the icy block that sat in her stomach, making it hard to pull in a full breath.

She stood with Ty by the carriage, but they didn't speak. They hadn't even looked at each other since Thomas had traded Bo away.

Bo approached Thomas and the two of them spoke too quietly for Kristi to make out the words that passed between them. Thomas's hand rested on the bigger man's shoulder. Bo's lowered head nodded every few seconds.

Kristi bit her lip. How could Thomas let this happen? How could she? Stephen had warned her not to meddle, not to try to change things in the past. He'd been right. They'd made things worse.

"What have we done?" she finally said to Ty.

He shook his head. "This is wrong, all wrong."

"So how do we fix it?"

"I don't know."

"Bo said Thomas has a plan."

Ty nodded. "It better be a good one."

Mackey came around the corner with the two boys. *Her* ancestors. They were why she'd come, why she'd traveled back in time. She should feel ecstatic at finding and helping to free them, not as if she'd been kicked in the gut and could barf all over the ground any second.

"Here you go," Mackey called, turning and shoving the smaller boy toward the carriage. The boy scuttled away from the man's reach.

The bigger one puffed out his chest, as if daring the man to shove him. Mackey ignored him. "Righ' this way, boy," he said, grabbing Bo's arm.

Bo jerked it away. He turned to face the man and glared so hard Kristi wondered if the look would burn a hole right through the slave catcher.

Mackey actually flinched. His fingers trembled as he groped for his whip. Thomas held up a hand and stepped between them. He touched Bo's shoulder and whispered something.

Bo nodded, unclenched his fists, then turned and walked away.

Mackey's lip curled into a snarl. He raised the whip over his shoulder.

"*Noo!*" Kristi gripped the sides of her head. He couldn't—but Mackey brought the whip down, ripping the knotted cords across Bo's back.

Bo gasped, stumbled, and hunched over for an instant. But after half a step, he threw his shoulders back and continued walking away, unbent.

TEN

Ty couldn't get his hands to stop shaking. All of this—of what had happened—was so *wrong*. He peered out the window as the carriage pulled away from the plantation, trying to catch another glimpse of Bo, but he was gone.

Ty glanced up at Thomas. The old man stared out the other window with red-rimmed eyes and a sunken, vacant look. The skin on his face looked looser, more lined and sallow. Ty bit his lip. Sure, he was upset. But how could he have left Bo with those monsters?

Kristi, on Ty's other side, shifted and wiped a tear from one cheek. Her eyes were red, too, hands clenched so tight her knuckles had gone pale as white marbles. Ty laid a hand over one of her clenched fists. She shook it off.

He sighed and looked across the carriage at the two boys. The older one was staring sullenly at the ceiling of the carriage, jaw clenched and a tendon quivering there. He clutched his knees with scarred, calloused hands.

The other boy's thin frame and slumped shoulders looked like he might fold in on himself, like a paper cutout. He trembled like a mouse trapped in a box, eyes darting as if searching for a way out.

After a silence that seemed to stretch for hours, Thomas let out a long-held breath. "Have no fear, boys. You're safe now."

Neither boy looked at him.

"My name is not Horace Humphries and I'm not from a plantation in Baltimore. I am Dr. Thomas Jordan and I have a home for freedmen in Pennsylvania with honest work for you. These are my friends, Kristi and Ty. We've come a long way to get the two of you."

The mousy one looked up for a split second, then at his brother. The other didn't stir. A rush of anger flushed in Ty's chest. Why were they so quiet? Did they know what Thomas had given up for them? What Bo had given up? Did they care at all?

"It's okay," Thomas said to Britt. "You have nothing to fear from us. Are you hungry?"

"He don't talk to no one but me, Massa," Jonah said, deep voice thick with resignation.

"I'm not your master, son. You're free now."

He looked up in bewilderment. "Free?"

Thomas nodded. He reached into his satchel and took out two documents. "I've told you true. I have the papers here. You're free men. Both of you."

Jonah eyed the papers skeptically, then took them and stuffed them into the waist of his pants. He looked up again, frowning. "But—why? Why you doin' this for us?"

Thomas's eyes twinkled. "Son, you wouldn't believe me if I told you."

* * *

Kristi stood in front of the inn, teeth chattering like the plastic, wind-up toy back home in her dentist's office. Gray clouds cast a dreary hue over the fields all around.

Thomas eased out of the carriage, grimacing with every move. Kristi didn't offer a helping hand, only moved away as Thomas went around to the front of the carriage to deal with the driver.

She turned and saw tendrils of smoke curling from the inn's chimney, warm candlelight glowing in the window. She wished *she* could spend the night curled in front of the fireplace, belly full of a good, heavy dinner.

She wrapped her arms about her and flinched when the clapboard walls of the stables shuddered and rattled in the wind. She shuddered, too, and hugged herself tighter. At least she had a coat. Neither Jonah nor Britt wore one, just long ragged shirts and pants cut off below the knees. Yet neither of them was shivering.

Ty nudged her. "You all right?"

"If turning into a human popsicle is *all right*, then I'm just peachy."

"I wish you could come inside, too," he said. "How about I stay out in the stables with you?"

"Don't be a prat," she said, rolling her eyes. "Go stay warm with the other white folks." She noticed Jonah was staring at her now, lip curled as if in disgust. What was his problem? It wasn't *her* fault they had to sleep out with the horses.

"Come on, Kristi," Ty said. "That's not fair."

"None of this is *fair*, Ty!" She turned her face from Jonah and lowered her voice to a harsh whisper. "It's all stupid! What's going to happen to Bo?"

"I don't know." Ty hesitated, then let out a long breath. "But Thomas won't leave him there. He *can't*. He'll think of something."

Kristi crossed her arms. "How am I supposed to go back to my time and pretend everything is all right when it's *my* fault Bo's a slave again?"

"It's not your fault, Kristi."

She snorted. "It *is*. I'm the one who talked you into coming here and meddled with history, messing things up, just like Stephen warned. But I *won't* leave Bo there."

"No, me either. We'll come up with a new scheme. We'll get him back."

"Then start thinking!" Kristi kicked a clump of dirt and stomped toward the rickety stables.

* * *

Ty lay on the bed, staring into the darkened eaves, listening to the sounds of Thomas's wheezing, sleeping breaths beside him. He tried closing his eyes and begged sleep to come, but the image of Mackey whipping Bo kept snapping his eyes open. Stephen had been right. Kristi too. It *was* their fault.

"We'll get you back, Bo," he whispered into the dark. "As God is my witness."

He took a deep breath and closed his eyes again, then heard a dog bark somewhere outside. His eyes snapped open. Another dog chimed in. He pushed the scratchy blanket off, went to the window, and saw circles of light bobbing in the darkness through the blurry pane.

"Thomas! Thomas! Wake up. Someone's outside."

The old man's eyes fluttered open. He looked around bleakly, as if he was unsure where he was.

"Come on," Ty urged. "Wake up!"

Thomas groaned and sat up. "What is it?"

"Lanterns outside."

Thomas grimaced, using his hands to guide one pale, skinny leg off the bed and onto the floor, then the other. He leaned forward, propped his head in his hands and chuckled ruefully. "My old bones aren't cooperating. How many?"

Ty went back to the window, counted the bobbing lights and silhouettes holding them. "Four. Something's not right. We have to warn Kristi."

"Go."

Ty crept into the hallway and down the stairs. The main room of the inn was dark. Embers smoked in the great fireplace. As he reached the landing, someone pounded from outside the front door, rattling the hinges.

He spun away to the hallway leading to the back way, but the glow of an oil lamp emerged from the innkeeper's room on the ground floor.

"I'm coming, I'm coming," the innkeeper called in a gruff voice as he crossed the room. His long white nightshirt stopped just above thin, hairy shins.

Ty stole back up the stairs and waited at the top, listening.

The innkeeper unbolted the door. The hinges creaked as the door swung open.

"What d'you all want?"

"There a Horace Humphries been boardin' here?"

"Mayhap," the innkeeper said. "What d'you want with him?"

"He's hiding runaways."

Ty bolted down the hall and burst back into his room. Thomas stood next to the bed, cane in one hand, bracing the small of his back with the other.

"They're looking for you!" Ty cried. "They said you're hiding runaways."

A shadow fell over Thomas's face. "Where's the time machine?"

"Here." Ty lifted his shirt to show the time rod tied to his waist with rope.

"Good. Take my wallet." He handed the folded, leather portfolio over and Ty tucked it into his pants. "Get out that window and go to the others," Thomas said. "Then get them out of here. Now!"

"Window? But—what do you mean? What about you?"

Thomas shook his head. "I'm too old to be crawling around rooftops."

"No! I—"

"The time to argue is over! Go!"

Ty hesitated, then went to the sash window and jammed it open. Icy wind blew in, stealing his breath. It was a moonless night out there, pitch black. He made out the overhanging roof about a foot beyond the window, ducked through and stepped onto the slippery slate shingles.

"Don't worry about me," Thomas said. "Get Kristi and the boys out of here. Take them to the harbor in Chestertown tomorrow and find Bo. He'll know what to do."

Heavy footsteps clomped up the stairs.

"Bo? What do you mean? He's at Conwell's. How am I supposed to—"

A heavy fist pounded on the door.

"*Go!*" Thomas closed the window. Ty crouched until his eyes were even with the sill, but didn't yet move away. The door burst open, ripping away from one hinge, hanging sideways. A huge man with a brown sack over his head entered.

Ty crawled toward the eaves and looked over, but couldn't see the ground through the dark. It was only about ten feet down, but the blackness made it appear a deep chasm.

He hung his legs over, took a deep breath, and dropped. His knees buckled when he landed and he fell back hard onto his rear. Gritting his teeth, he scrambled to the wall of the inn and slid toward the front. Four horses were tied to the post around the corner.

"Come on outta here," called a gruff voice from the stables.

"Get off me!" Kristi screamed. "Let go!"

Ty crouched to conceal himself behind the horses, but peered out through their legs. Another man with a sack over his head held a bull's eye lantern in one hand and dragged Kristi from the stables by her arm with the other. He threw her to the ground. Two more followed, dragging Jonah and Britt. The last man carried a flaming torch.

Ty petted the neck of the nervously-sidling horse to sooth it, then dug in the saddlebag and found a long hunting knife. He pulled off the sheath and cut the straps under the horse's belly. He ducked under the horse and did the same to the second saddle. On the third horse, his hand groped across the cold metal barrel of a shotgun. He loosed it from the scabbard, then cut the straps on the last two horses and returned to the darkness against the inn's wall. Cradling the gun across his chest, he made his way around to the back of the stables and slid through the open door. He went to the front and peered through the slats.

Kristi, Jonah, and Britt were now kneeling with their hands on top of their heads. The three men stood over them. One aimed a shotgun aimed at Jonah's chest.

"Y'all didn't get too far, did you?"

A sick feeling squeezed Ty's stomach. The man pulled off the sack, revealing the familiar scraggly beard, and long, crooked nose.

Mackey!

Ty clenched his fists around the barrel of the shotgun. He narrowed his eyes and lifted the gun, aiming it through the slat at the slave catcher's chest. He could end this now. Shoot Mackey and send the others scattering. Then Kristi and the others could escape. Trembling, he slid a finger onto the trigger. Sweat dripped into his eyes. He blinked the salt burn away and tried to slow his breathing, to aim the sight at the center of the slave catcher's chest.

He's a bad guy. He deserves it!

But his finger wouldn't tighten, as if it doubted this.

"Bloody hell!" He lowered the gun.

"Miss me, boys?" Mackey drawled, smirking. "Tol' you I'd be seein' you soon."

"Let us go!" Kristi cried. "They're free now. You can't—"

"Shut up, girl!"

The man who'd burst into their room came out of the inn, pushing another in front of him. Thomas, who had a gash above his right eyebrow. The blood made him look deathly pale.

"Thought you'd get away with stealin' Mr. Conwell's property," Mackey shouted. "We oughta string you up right here."

"Those boys are mine and you know it," Thomas said. "I paid what Conwell asked. Go on and get the marshal. I've stolen nothing."

Mackey raised his eyebrows and looked up at the man behind Thomas. "You find the papers?"

"He ain't got 'em," the man said.

"I sent them with the mail coach," Thomas said. "They'll be in my lawyer's hands by morning, if you want to look at them. Then you might want to inquire about his fee. You're going to need a lawyer."

Mackey's eyes narrowed. "You're lyin'." He grabbed a hold of Britt's shirt. "Where're them papers, boy?"

Britt shook like a sheet hanging in a windstorm. A wet stain darkened the front of his trousers.

"Tell me where you hid 'em!" The slave catcher pulled one fist back. "Or I'll—"

"Let 'im go," Jonah yelled, jumping up. One of the others kicked him in the stomach. Jonah gasped and went down. The tail of his shirt came free, showing the papers tucked into his waistband.

"Well, would you look at that," Mackey said, dropping Britt, who fell in a heap next to his brother. Mackey snatched up the papers. "Good. That's real good." He looked up at the man holding the torch. "Bring that over here." Mackey held the edge to the flame.

"*No!*" Kristi yelled.

The papers darkened, then a hole ate through the center and spread. Mackey grinned and dropped the flaming paper onto the ground.

Jonah's face hardened. Tears rolled from Kristi's eyes.

"Now y'all can come down to N'awlins with me. Smart girl like you, strong boy like him, always fetch a nice price." He sneered at Britt, who still lay in a heap on the ground. "Heck, even the sniveling worm might be worth a few dollars."

A fifth man approached behind the others. He was bigger than the rest and still had the burlap bag over his head.

Ty's forehead wrinkled. Where'd this guy come from? There'd only been four horses. The others didn't seem to notice the new one.

"Get some rope," Mackey ordered.

Ty aimed the shotgun again. He had to act, *now*! He tensed his finger and pulled the trigger. An explosion roared in his ears and the stock punched his shoulder, knocking him backward. He sat stunned, ears ringing. The shot had apparently sailed over the heads of the men, but it sent them diving for cover.

All but the biggest. He lurched forward, grabbing Kristi with one hand and Britt with the other, dragging them back toward the stable. Jonah reached out, but the big man shrugged him off and kicked the door open.

Ty lifted the shotgun toward the man's chest. He pulled the trigger again.

Click. And again. Nothing.

The man knocked the barrel aside and yanked the sack off his head. "You trying to shoot me, boy?" A dark face beamed at Ty.

"B—Bo?" Ty gasped. "Wh—how did you—what the heck—"

Jonah charged in and wrenched Britt from Bo's grasp. "Who're you?"

"No time." Bo slammed the door and leaned against it. "The first man to show his face gets it blown off!" he shouted.

Ty shook his head. "I don't have any more shells."

Bo smiled. "They don't know that."

Outside, Mackey's angry voice rose. "They can't shoot us all. Go on, get in there! You two, go 'round back!"

"I ain't steppin' in front of that door!" another voice answered.

Mackey swore. "Burn 'em out, then!"

The torch flew in the window and lit the straw on the floor. Smoke filled the structure. The horses kicked against the stall doors.

"Run out the back," Bo ordered, coughing. "Run 'til you can't run anymore."

"But they're out there," Ty said, pulling his shirt over his mouth.

Bo unlatched all the stall doors, stepping back as each horse pushed out. He grabbed the halter of the first and guided it toward the open back door. The other two followed.

"Go on behind 'em!"

The horses trampled the men standing outside. Ty pulled Kristi's arm, dragging her out into the sweet, fresh air, past the men on the ground, and across the dark field. Bo, Jonah, and Britt were close behind.

Halfway across, Ty hazarded a look back. He saw a man swing onto one of the horses with the cut saddle straps, then slide off.

They ran toward the silhouettes of black trees marking the edge of the field. Just as they reached the edge of the woods, Ty stopped and yanked Kristi back. "Wait! What about Thomas?"

Bo moved past without slowing. "Thomas knows what he's about."

"But we can't leave him with them!" Ty yelled, chasing the man.

"Thomas has gotten himself out of bigger messes than this."

"I'm not leaving him!" He grabbed Bo's arm and he stopped.

"They *will* string you up for stealing slaves if they catch you, Ty," Bo said.

"They don't know I'm with you," Ty said. "So I can help Thomas."

"Me too," Kristi said.

Ty shook his head. "No, stay with Bo. You heard what Mackey said about selling you in New Orleans."

"No time for bickering," Bo said. "Keep moving. There'll be dogs before long."

"Then stop arguing!" Ty jerked his arm free. "I'm going back."

"We can't split up!" Kristi cried. "What about the time machine?"

Ty untied the rod from his waist. "Here, take it. Use it to get out of here if you have to."

"That won't help the others," she said.

"Give it here." Bo took the time machine. "When you find Thomas, tell him we've gone to find some *Friends*."

Kristi grabbed Ty's hand. "I don't want to leave you!"

"Just go." He squeezed her trembling hand. "I'll get Thomas, then we'll catch up."

"Come on, girl." Bo put a hand on her shoulder. "We have to run."

"This is stupid, Ty! You *know* it is."

"Yeah. But I can't let Thomas get hurt."

She hugged him, squeezing until he wheezed. "Be safe," she whispered.

He hugged back. "*You* be safe. Don't get caught."

She squeezed him one more time, then bolted off after the three runaways who were already disappearing in the trees.

ELEVEN

Kristi plodded behind the dark shapes of the others, her feet like blocks of ice. She had no idea how far they'd run, sloshing for miles up the center of a frigid, knee-deep creek, crossing field after frozen field.

The initial excitement of the escape had blown away in the frosty wind that chilled her core, but burned her lungs. With it went the rush of adrenaline that'd made her feel she could sprint for hours.

There'd been a horse, the one Bo had stolen from Conwell's plantation and ridden to their rescue. She thought of that mare now, wishing she were sitting on its back. But Bo had sent it off riderless hours earlier, a ploy to confuse their pursuers.

Her mind wandered toward food: steaming hot chocolate and buttery buns right from the oven. Her stomach rumbled. Food would help. Her last chance at a *meal*, if you could call it that, had been the hard bread and watery stew Ty had brought after they'd returned from Conwell's. Jonah and Britt hadn't minded the stew. Obviously they'd learned to expect nothing better. But Kristi rejected it on principle. She'd pictured the white people in the inn getting fat on roast beef and potatoes and pastries while sending only the scraps to the *servants* in the stables. Ty hadn't looked her in the eyes when he'd brought it, confirming her suspicions. "I'd rather starve," she'd said.

And now maybe she would.

She looked up again, straining her eyes to find the dark shapes ahead. Jonah and Britt moved silently, without complaint, while her every step was a struggle. She gritted her teeth. Why was she always the one who had to suffer?

"I need to rest," she called out, stopping to lean against a tree.

"Just a couple hours 'til daylight," Bo called back.

Kristi slid down the tree and sat anyway. "My legs are falling off, so unless you plan on carrying me, I have to sit. Just for a minute."

Jonah grumbled something she couldn't make out.

"There's no one back there anyway," she said. "They're probably all still toasting next to a fire, waiting for sunrise to come after us."

"Five minutes," Bo finally agreed.

Kristi leaned her head back against the rough bark and closed her eyes. Jonah and Britt squatted a little way off, but Bo came to sit next to her.

"Where'd you come from, anyway?" she asked him. "How'd you get away?"

He smiled. "All part of Thomas's grand scheme."

"Yeah, you said he had a plan. What was it?"

"You see, this is the third time Thomas has sold me off." He chuckled. "But I keep coming back. Haven't spent a whole night as a slave since I was a boy." His voice swelled with pride.

"Sold you off? Do you mean Thomas *knew* Conwell would want you in exchange for Britt and Jonah?"

Bo nodded. "Thomas comes to them as a small-time planter, desperate to grow at any cost. The big-time planters smell that desperation and take advantage, blinded by their greed. He never *offers* me, but reluctantly agrees when they press. Conwell was no different. I was supposed to wait 'til dark, then run off and meet you at the harbor tomorrow. But we didn't count on those fellas coming after you. I saw them saddling up and knew what they were gonna do. So I waited 'til they left, stole another of Conwell's horses, and followed."

"But why would Conwell sell Jonah and Britt just to steal them back?"

"Conwell probably didn't know anything about it. Some Wolves like Mackey make extra money kidnapping freedmen and selling them down in Mississippi or Alabama."

"That's horrible!"

Bo snorted. "What about slavery *isn't*?"

"I know." She sighed. "So now what?"

"Them Wolves'll figure on us running north, toward a free state. Pennsylvania's closest. But we'll head for Delaware. Thomas'll look for us in Wilmington. We have Friends there."

"Friends? Who?"

"Quakers. Some of them are on the underground."

"You mean the Underground Railroad?"

He nodded.

"Just like Harriet Tubman. Those men in the stables said she was around here. Maybe we'll meet her."

Bo laughed. "Nobody just *meets* Ol' Moses. She's a phantom. A wraith."

"Wow." Kristi leaned back. "Ty's not going to believe this."

"If we live, you can tell him all about it. But there's a long road to travel." He stood and held a hand out.

She gripped it and stood. Her legs hurt more now than they had before they'd rested. But she trudged along, biting back complaints, working hard to stay just behind Bo and ahead of Jonah and Britt.

The hours wore on with only the shuffle of their footsteps through sand and across frozen fields. No one spoke. Each seemed only able to concentrate on his own exhaustion.

Eventually black sky paled to somber gray. The silhouettes of barren trees sharpened, branches clawing at the sky like gnarled, desperate fingers.

Somewhere a bird chirped. Then another.

Kristi glanced back and saw the top of Britt's head as he stumbled along, chin on chest. His shoulders were slumped, his arms swung loosely.

"You all right, Britt?"

He stopped and looked up quickly, as if startled awake, then dropped his head again. His shoulders slumped even farther.

She stopped too, and turned to him. "Are you okay?"

Jonah stepped between them. "Let 'im alone."

"I'm just talking to him, Jonah. What's wrong with that?"

"He ain't gonna talk to you. Jus' go away."

"Why?"

"'Cuz he don' talk to no one but me!"

"Why not?"

"'Cuz he don't!"

She scowled. "What's your problem, anyway?"

He shoved past without answering, but she grabbed his arm.

"I'm just trying to help. You don't have to be so mean."

He ripped his arm from her grasp. "How's a white man's pet gonna help us?"

"What're you talking about? I'm nobody's pet!"

"No?" He glared. "You ever been whipped?"

"What's that got to do with anything?"

"Ever been beat with a stick?" His voice was tight with contempt.

"*No*. So what?"

"I seen you throwin' fits 'cuz the food ain't good enough. 'Cuz you gotta sleep out with the *slaves*. Well, bein' a pet don' make you no better than us."

She stepped back, feeling slapped. "I—I'm just trying to help," she muttered around a lump in her throat.

"Then keep your mouth closed and let us alone!"

She suddenly felt Bo at her shoulder.

"No time for this," he said. "We're all tired, but you gotta keep moving."

She stepped aside, hoping it was still dark enough to hide the tears filling her eyes. Jonah stomped past and Britt followed, gaze on the ground.

"Don't worry about him," Bo said.

"But why does he *hate* me?"

"He's just looking out for his brother. We're all in this—"

An eerie howl floated to them from a distance. Icy pinpricks ran up the back of Kristi's neck. She shook her head, hoping it'd just been her imagination, or a stray, or—

But Bo stiffened and clamped her arm, hand like a vise.

"*Run!*"

And, forgetting all the insults, pain, hunger, and exhaustion she'd thought she'd felt, Kristi bolted, running for her life.

* * *

Ty spent most of the night freezing, perched up in a tree overlooking the inn. He'd crept back, circling the burning stables, ready for the moment when Mackey and his men would finally come charging out in pursuit of Kristi and the others.

But they never came.

Warily, he'd climbed the tree and kept watch from a thick bough halfway up. It seemed Mackey and his men were gone. Thomas, too. They couldn't have gone after Kristi and the others yet; he'd have seen them.

The innkeeper and two other men fought the flames with buckets of water. It'd occurred to Ty that he could help, that another hand may have made a difference. But it was way too risky. Mackey might return and see him. In the end, the fire reduced the stables to a smoldering heap of ashes. The soot-smeared innkeeper had thrown down his pail and stormed into the inn, cursing the runaways, as if all of this had been *their* fault.

When all was finally quiet, Ty's eyelids grew heavy. He wedged himself between trunk and branches and fought to stay awake. But sleep overtook him almost as soon as he'd settled in.

Three hours later, the baying of a hound startled him awake. He jerked sideways, throwing his arms around the branch to keep from crashing through. Righting himself, he shook his head, groggy and disoriented. All he could see in the dark was the glow of embers that used to be the stable building.

Another long, chilling howl. Ty peered toward the sound and saw a line of bobbing lights in the distance. As they closed in, he counted ten bull's eye lanterns. Most seemed to be carried by men on horseback. After them came three men on foot, gripping taut leashes behind the bloodhounds.

"Well, here they come." He ran a hand through his hair. "Hope you're long gone, Kristi."

The group stopped at the inn. Two men dismounted. One banged on the inn's door. The other stood on the doorstep and turned to look over the wide fields. Mackey. Ty closed his eyes and sighed. How had Mackey been able to rouse such a big posse? Surely so many men couldn't have been in on Mackey's plot, which amounted to kidnapping.

The innkeeper came down and flung the door open, cursing. Mackey backhanded him and he fell silent.

Then, the man who'd knocked on the door shoved Mackey and the two of them yelled back and forth at each other. Ty leaned forward, straining his ears to hear what they were saying, but the only words he made out was the other man yelling, "...and Charles ain't even been killed!"

Killed? What had Mackey told them?

While the men argued, the dog handlers let the bloodhounds sniff around the smoldering ruins. Near what had been the back door, all three lifted their muzzles, bayed in chorus, and pulled at their leashes.

"Bloody hell," Ty whispered. They'd found the scent.

Mackey remounted and called to the others, waving his lantern. The dogs were loosed, but only three men followed. The man Mackey had been arguing with remounted as well, but turned his horse and went back the way he'd come. The remaining others followed him.

When all the men from the fractured posse had disappeared from sight, Ty climbed down and ran to the inn. The innkeeper could tell him what had happened to Thomas. He climbed the steps and banged on the door.

A minute later, the oil-lamp glow lit the cracks and the latch rattled.

"What is it now?" growled the innkeeper as he swung the door open. A gray, handlebar mustache framed his sharp chin. Soot still smudged his chin and bald pate and his cheek was red from where Mackey had hit him. He looked down on Ty and the rest of his face reddened. "*You!*"

"I'm really sorry about your stables, sir," Ty said, holding a hand up. "It wasn't us who—"

The innkeeper thrust his face at him. "Go sit on your sorry. Git on outta here or I'll really *make* you sorry!"

"Please, sir." Ty backed down the steps. "What did they do with Thom—with my granddad?"

The innkeeper waved dismissively. "Strung 'im up, for all I care. How will I serve my guests with no stables for their horses?"

"I am sorry about that. Truly. But my grandfather can help you. Please, just tell me where he is. They didn't hurt him, did they?"

"I don't care what they did with him!"

"I'm telling you, my granddad *will* pay for your trouble. He's quite well off."

"Well off, is he?" The man's face suddenly softened and, as in Conwell's eyes earlier that day, Ty imagined dollar signs replacing his shining pupils. He scratched his sooty chin. "It'll cost at least five-hundred dollars to rebuild my stables."

"My granddad is good for it. I promise. But first, I must find him. Where'd they take him?"

The innkeeper scoffed. "I don't want your promises, boy. I want a *promissory note.*"

"I don't have time for this!"

"Then good luck findin' him on your own. There's thousands of trees out there." He drew his hand across the horizon. "He could be strung up in any one of 'em."

"Fine," Ty grumbled. "Write up a bloody note."

The keeper went back into the inn, returning five minutes later with a note and pen. Ty glanced at the note and smiled inwardly. According to the script, Horace Humphries would pay Charles Atwater five-hundred dollars. He did feel a little guilty about cheating the innkeeper, who had, after all, done nothing wrong and had the right to be angry about his stables being burned down. But there was nothing Ty could do about that now, so he signed the note *Ty Humphries* and handed it back. "So where'd they take him."

"To the marshal in Chestertown."

"Thank you, sir. How far is that?"

"Five miles down that road." He pointed over Ty's head.

"Thank you, sir." He lit out without another word.

The road walk was long, cold, and quiet, twisting and turning between flat fields. He slid his arms into his sleeves. Still cold. He stuffed his hands into his armpits. His fingers felt like frozen hot dogs, even through his shirt.

After an hour or so of trudging along, the first hints of dawn turned the clouds pink. But, instead of getting warmer, the air seemed to sharpen and grow even colder. He wrapped his arms around his body and hugged himself, teeth chattering. A bird chirped in a tree off to one side of the road. Another answered. Ty looked up and spotted a small, dark outline among the branches.

Ah, breakfast time, he thought ruefully and rubbed his stomach. *Could go for some hot biscuits and a whole pot of tea with sugar.*

He passed a few farmhouses, three or four one-story structures and a few larger spreads farther off the road, smoke curling from brick chimneys. Ty's mouth watered when the wind brought the scent of frying bacon from one of the smaller farmhouses. *Wonder if they'd invite a weary traveler to breakfast*, he mused. But he had to keep moving.

Finally, the sun burned the clouds away, rising above the trees ahead, inching into a clear, blue sky. The temperature seemed nearly as cold as the night before, but he suddenly felt warmer, more energized, remembering the cold winter mornings he'd spent spreading fertilizer on Stephen's farm. Back then the same feeling of warmth and energy had jolted him when the sun had cleared the horizon and smiled down. Something about bright rays on his face cut the bitterest chill.

A few miles later came the *clop-clop* of shod hooves and crunching of wooden wheels on the crushed shells covering the road. He spun and saw a flatbed wagon drawn by a mule rounding the bend.

Empty fields lay on either side with no trees to duck behind. Besides, the driver was already close enough to have seen him. So Ty stepped off the road to wait for the wagon to pass.

As it rumbled closer, he saw the driver was an older black man with a close-cut U of gray hair around a bald pate. Thick, leathery wrinkles creased his face, like lines in a favorite pair of shoes.

"Mornin'," the driver called, reining in his mule. His lips seemed caved in, and Ty guessed he had no teeth left. A jumble of split logs filled the bed of the wagon.

"Good morning," Ty said, bowing slightly. "This the way to Chestertown?"

The man nodded. "Goin' dat way, if'n you care to ride along."

Ty considered his aching legs. "Yes, sir. I would."

"*Suh?*" The man laughed and slapped a skinny thigh. "You ain't from 'round here, is you?"

Ty grinned. "No, sir."

"Well, git on up, den, young suh. Name's Elias." He scooted to make room on the seat next to him.

Ty climbed up. "My name's Ty."

Elias flicked the reins and they were off.

"Whatchoo doin' walkin' out so early in de mornin'?" Elias asked.

"Just headed to Chestertown to meet my grandfather."

"You ain't had nothin' to do wit' dat hubbub at Mista Charles' Inn las' nigh'?"

Ty stiffened. My, word traveled fast here, even without cell phones and internet. "What hubbub?"

"Hear tell some runaways kilt Mista Charles and all de people stayin' dere, den burnt de place down."

Ty bit his lip and shifted uneasily. "No, I hadn't heard."

"Half o' Chestertown be out looking foah 'em."

Ty gritted his teeth. That's why so many men had come back with Mackey. How many others had gone off in different directions? And that's why Mackey and that man had argued at the inn, when they'd found Charles alive and the inn still standing.

"You's lookin' mighty pale, boy. Like you seen a ghost."

"Just tired," Ty said, forcing a smile.

Elias dug in a poke sack between his feet, withdrew a square of cornbread, and held it out.

"You's welcome to it," he said. "My missus packed it, but ain't wort' de trouble chawin' wit' dese gums." He grinned toothlessly.

"Thanks." Ty crunched into the square, which was bland and chewed like granola, but it softened as he worked it around his mouth and then went down easily enough. He wondered how Elias could have possibly gotten it down without teeth.

"How much farther to Chestertown?"

"Mile or so."

"Can you take me to the jailhouse?"

"De jailhouse?" The man looked startled. "Thought you was lookin' for yoah gran'daddy."

"That's right."

"Okay, den." Elias shrugged. He flicked the reins and the mule looked back sullenly. The road curved along a small creek, which soon joined with others to form a small river. Large, brick homes and farmhouses dotted the river's banks. Men were out, chopping wood, feeding chickens and pigs, pulling fishing nets into small boats. They passed a girl about Ty's age in a long wool skirt and a straw hat pumping water from a spigot into a pail. She glanced, meeting Ty's curious gaze. He nodded and she blushed, lowering her head again.

The gaps between houses lessened, until they came to a small wooden sign that read *Chestertown, est. 1706.* Two-story houses lined the main street, set between taverns and shops. Men wore wool trousers and frockcoats nipped at the waist. Women wore colorful cotton dresses with capes and thin, white gloves and bonnets.

"Lots of money in Chestertown?" Ty asked.

Elias nodded. "Busiest port in Mar'lan', 'cept Annapolis."

The wagon went down a side street and past a small church. The sign in front read *St. Paul's* and had a carving of a bearded man with a gilded halo. The great brick building had a pitched roof, arched windows and doorway. A wide graveyard lay behind it, full of marble stones and wooden crosses.

Past the church was another brick building, boxy and short. The windows were square with vertical bars over them. Tall, wooden stocks with holes just big enough to trap a head and two hands stood in front. They were empty and Ty let out a breath of relief. Thomas couldn't have survived a cold night clamped in stocks.

Elias reined the mule to a stop in front of the jailhouse. "Well, here you be, young suh. Hope yoah gran'daddy be all right."

Yeah, me too, Ty thought, but only said, "He's a tough old coot." He hopped down. "Thank you, Elias."

"No trouble, foah a boy who call me suh." He flashed that toothless grin. "*Suh*. If dat don't beat all." He laughed as the wagon pulled away.

Ty glanced up at the jailhouse and sighed. *Now what?*

He still had Thomas's purse. Maybe he could bribe the jailer—or maybe the jailer would just take the money and arrest him, too.

He chuckled. If Kristi was here, she'd come up with some half-cocked scheme to blow out a wall and escape with Thomas before the dust settled. But no dynamite lay about, so he'd go with plan B, whatever that was. But what if the innkeeper was wrong? Thomas might not even be in there.

All right, Ty. Think.

He slipped around the side of the building to a window and looked over the sill. In a small room on the other side, an old man was snoring in a wooden arm chair, feet up on the desk. Keys hung from a ring on the wall above his head. Ty ducked and went around to the back wall, where two barred windows were set. The first cell was empty, but the second was too dark to see anything. He listened, but didn't hear any movement, either.

Where are you Thom—

A raspy cough came from inside the dark cell.

"Thomas?" Ty whispered. "*Thomas?*"

A groan, then the creaking of metal. "Ty. Is that you?"

"Yes! You okay?"

Thomas laughed and then coughed again. "Oh, I've been better." His voice came closer. Ty could see a faint figure in the dark. "Where're the others?"

"Ran off last night. Bo came back and helped them escape. He said to tell you he's going to find friends."

"Good, good. You still have that money?"

Ty patted the leather pouch in his waistband. "Right here."

"Listen carefully. Buy a ticket onto a ship going north to Elkton, then take a train to Wilmington, Delaware. I've a friend there, a man by the name of Thomas Garrett. He owns an iron and hardware shop. Tell him who you are, and of Kristi and the others' plight. He'll help."

Ty gripped the bars. "Why tell me this, Thomas? I came to get *you* out. I can find some tools to dig these bars out, no problem. We can *both* go to Wilmington."

"No time to wait on a doddering old man. My jailhouse escape days are long behind me."

Ty's throat constricted. "But they might hang you."

Thomas laughed. "I may be old and sickly, but I still have use of my Jordan wiles, brother. Now *go*."

Ty reached through the bars into the darkness. He felt Thomas's hand, the weakness in the grip, the brittle feeling of those thin fingers.

"I'll get them," Ty said. "Then come back for you."

"I know," Thomas said, squeezing his hand. "Now go."

Ty stood, wiped the tears from the corners of his eyes, and stole away from the jailhouse.

* * *

As Ty turned the corner and raced away from the jailhouse, two men emerged from the doorway of St. Paul's and followed him down the street.

TWELVE

Kristi tore across the open field, pursued by the baying of hounds. Cold and exhaustion forgotten, she ran with every bit of energy left in her. She imagined dogs the size of ponies, snarling at her heels. Huge, cruel men with tobacco-stained teeth shooting them down. She thought of an iron collar and chains around her neck. Of whips flaying her back. She ran even faster.

She glimpsed Britt's small form darting ahead in the half-light. Gone was the sluggish, sloped gait. Now he was a swift fawn fleeing a hungry pack.

She veered left and ran into the woods. Briars tore at her face and arms. She flailed at the vines and jumped exposed roots.

Another chorus of howls rang out, closer.

On Britt's heels, she emerged from the trees to the bank of a river. The trees on the far side were thicker.

"Take this!" Bo ordered, shoving the time rod into her hands. "Get out of here while you can."

The cold metal chilled her hands. Now she pictured her bedroom at home. Could almost feel the down comforter wrapped around her. Her mother and father.

Derek and Sarah. Even her stupid school and boring classes...

She could go back now, be safe. She could take the others with her, just form the halo, grab arms and— poof—gone to where no slave catcher could ever follow. What would it be like for them to suddenly jump forward 150 years to a time *without* slavery in our country?

No. Don't be stupid! What would happen to her family tree if Jonah wasn't here to start it? Would the rest of her family even exist? Would she?

She shook the thought away and looked up. Jonah was glaring at her. He couldn't know what the time machine was or what it could do. But clearly he thought she was thinking of leaving them, somehow, by the contempt on his face. Expecting her to run off, to forsake them and save herself. *White man's pet.*

She gritted her teeth. "I'm not going anywhere!" She shoved the rod back into Bo's hands and glared back at Jonah. "I'm *not* leaving any of you behind!"

Bo stripped off his shirt. "We have to cross. Can you swim?"

She looked over the river. It was slow moving, but wide—about fifty yards across. She shivered. "Y-yes."

He turned to Britt and Jonah. "Can you swim?"

Jonah shook his head.

Bo swore softly and scanned the bank. "Well, we gotta try to cross. It's just an inlet, shouldn't be too deep. "Take off your clothes." He pulled off his pants.

Kristi averted her eyes. "Why?"

"We'll freeze in half an hour in wet clothes. Take 'em off. Keep 'em dry."

Kristi stood horrified as Jonah and Britt stripped.

"Ain't no time to be bashful, girl," Bo said. "They're coming."

Escaping with the time machine suddenly sounded like a viable option. "But—but—"

More howls and yips cut through the air. With a moan, she stripped off her coat and dress, but held them to cover herself. Bo stepped into the water, followed by Jonah, then Britt, and Kristi last. The icy water numbed her feet to the ankles. Bo pushed ahead until the water was waist deep, then to his chest. Her legs soon went numb. Her breath came in short gasps that couldn't seem to fill her lungs. Her arms quivered, as if she held a bowling ball over her head instead of a flimsy dress. By halfway across, the water was to her neck and the current made her stagger.

They were nearly to the other side, entering shallower depths, when Britt stumbled. He went down with a great splash. Jonah lunged to grab him, but the boy disappeared under the surface.

"Britt!" Jonah thrashed over to the spot his brother went down. After a few seconds that felt like as many hours, Britt broke the surface—but well beyond Jonah's reach. His skinny arms flailed, he coughed and gasped.

"Put your feet down!" Kristi screamed, but he kept floundering, drifting away.

She dropped her clothes and dove after him. The frigid water seemed to fight her, but she planted her feet against the mucky bottom, shoved up, and caught the current. She stroked ahead until her splayed fingers brushed something solid and slippery. A leg! Britt thrashed, grabbing her arm with a petrified strength that threatened to drown both of them. Her lungs screamed and she saw bright flashes of stars. She rolled over and kicked to break his grip. As it loosened, she wrenched free, grabbed his arm, and pulled him to the surface.

They emerged, sputtering and coughing. Her feet found the riverbed again.

"Here!" Bo called, reaching a hand.

She grabbed it and he hauled them toward the bank, where she sprawled out on the cold sand, suddenly exhausted, and coughed and sputtered. "B-Britt?" she muttered.

"He's okay," Bo said, motioning with his head.

She turned her head slightly, saw Britt sitting in the dirt, hugging his knees to his chest. Jonah knelt behind him, rubbing his shoulders. Jonah looked up, caught her eyes, and nodded.

Instead of cold, her skin felt like it was on fire. She suddenly felt her nakedness.

"M-my clothes."

"Washed away," Bo said, laying his shirt over her.

"Thanks." She guided quivering arms into the sleeves.

"We gotta keep moving," he said.

She nodded and stood, wavering on legs that felt like bent saplings. The shirt draped to her mid thighs.

The baying of the dogs came again, but now from across the river. Farther away. They climbed a hill and looked down on a valley below.

"Get down," Bo ordered and they pressed flat against the ground and peered through a spiny bush. At the foot of the hill, in a small field, a draft horse was hitched to a wagon. A bearded man in suspenders and a round-brimmed straw hat stood behind the wagon, shoveling something onto the field. The heavy black beard covered his cheeks and chin, but his upper lip was shaved clean.

In her own time, she'd often seen such men on trips to her Mimi's, even sometimes in the small towns outside of Philadelphia, driving big black horse-drawn buggies alongside of the roads instead of cars and trucks.

"Oh—Is he Amish?"

Bo shook his head. "Quaker. He may help us. Stay here." He stood.

Kristi grabbed his arm. "Wait. What if he tries to catch us? He might keep slaves, too."

"You think he'd be working his own field if he had slaves?" Bo laughed. "Quakers don't abide slavery, whether they're on the underground or not."

"But—"

He cut her off. "You could still freeze to death. We all might. We gotta find warm shelter, dry cloths, and food."

Without giving her the chance to argue further, he descended the hill. The farmer looked up as Bo emerged from the trees.

Bo approached, hands open in front of him. The farmer paused and greeted him. They talked for a minute, then Bo pointed up the hill. The farmer nodded and Bo waved. "Come on down," he called, smiling.

* * *

The main room of the farmer's small house was no bigger than Kristi's own bedroom back home. Two wooden chairs and a spinning wheel sat before the hearth. Behind those was a wooden table, four more chairs, and a large cupboard. The only decoration was a wooden cross hung from a nail on the wall.

Only the roaring fire in the hearth drew Kristi's interest. She rushed to it and held her hands over the crackling flames, elbowing for position with Jonah and Britt. The farmer disappeared into another room. A few minutes later, a yawning woman in a flannel nightgown and long black hair in a braid emerged with quilts clutched in her arms. She wrapped the quilts around each of them and said, "Sit. Warm thyselves."

Kristi clutched the quilt to her. "Th-thank you, ma'am."

"My name is Clara. My husband is Johann," the woman said and touched Kristi's head. She was young with plain features, but her bright blue eyes shone when she smiled. "You are safe, now."

Clara gave them crusty rye bread and bowls of thick rabbit stew. But it took a long time for Kristi's teeth to stop chattering enough to eat.

When she was finally warm and had a full belly, the previous night's exhaustion fell on her like an anvil. She slept at the fireplace fender for hours.

When she finally stirred, it was dark outside the kitchen window. Britt and Jonah lay a few feet away, still sleeping.

With a great yawn, she sat up and rubbed her hip, which felt bruised after being pressed against the hard floor. Her muscles ached as if she'd played five soccer games the day before. She sighed. *If only.*

She looked down on Britt. His face was a picture of peace. Gone were the tight lines of worry he had when awake. She marveled: he *was* just a *little boy. He* was the reason she came back. To save him. She smiled. All the pain was worth it!

Bo sat at the table with the farmer and his wife, candle between them as they leaned together whispering.

Kristi started to let the quilt around her shoulders slide to the floor, then remembered she wore only Bo's shirt under it. What a sight she must've been to Johann and Clara: exhausted, starved, half-naked and practically an ice cube. She wrapped the quilt around her carefully and stepped over Britt and Jonah.

Clara smiled as Kristi approached. "Do you feel restored?"

Kristi nodded. "Uh...yes. Thank you, Miss...Mrs. Clara."

"Come," the woman said, taking her hand. "I shall find you proper garments."

Kristi looked at Bo, who nodded.

Clara lit another candle from the one on the table and Kristi followed her from the room. The next room was smaller, with just a mission-style bed and a chest of drawers and wardrobe of raw wood. A white wool dress was laid out on the bed, identical to the one Clara wore. Beside it lay a gray hooded cape and woolen shawl. Kristi groaned inwardly, but supposed that her asking for pants instead would be out of the question.

Clara handed her a pair of leather shoes. "These will do?" she asked.

Kristi forced a smile. "Yes, thank you."

Clara put the candle on the chest and left the room. Sighing, Kristi slipped the dress over her head. It fit loosely and itched like crazy, but at least it would be warm. She bent and squeezed her feet into the shoes. Too tight, but better than tramping over the cold ground in bare feet. She ran her hands down the scratchy fabric, then picked up the cape and shawl and returned to the main room.

Jonah was up, standing by the table next to Bo and Clara. She went to sit with Britt by the fire. The boy glanced at her, then dropped his eyes to the coals.

"We must depart before the night grows old," Johann said. He led Bo, Britt, and Jonah into the small room.

Kristi watched Clara move about the cupboards and drop bread and dried meats into a white sack.

The others returned from the bedroom a few minutes later, garbed in thick gray woolen shirts and dark pants. Only Britt wore shoes, which looked about three sizes too big for him.

They quickly ate more of the rabbit stew, then Johann opened the door and a cold wind blew through the house, sending a chill up the backs of Kristi's legs. She drew the cape around her shoulders and lifted the hood.

Clara handed Bo the sack, looked them all over and nodded. "May God be with you on your journey."

"Thank you, Mrs. Clara," Kristi said and followed the others into the night. A half-moon perched high, casting enough light for her to see the outlines of trees surrounding the farm.

Johann led them across the field and into the trees. Nobody talked. Kristi kept alert for barking or howls, but only heard the sigh of the wind.

It wasn't long before the cold earth worked through her thin shoes and made her feet ache, then worked its way up her legs.

Great, she thought. *Here we go again.*

Where were Ty and Thomas and how were they going to find them? What about her dad and the wedding? A knot twisted in her stomach. She'd been so rude to him. He didn't deserve that. Even if he was marrying a woman who laughed like a chipmunk and had a snooping daughter who thought she was a princess.

"*Stop it!*" she grumbled, shaking her head. Jonah, who was only a few paces ahead, turned. His face screwed up, as if she'd been talking to him.

She opened her mouth to lash out at him, to tell him how ungrateful he was for everything she was trying to do for him and Britt when it hit her.

He thinks I'm a brat. He'd said as much when he'd accused her of throwing a fit for being lumped with the slaves. *White man's pet.*

She felt the blood rise to her head. How dare he—

Then she saw Britt, loping ahead, shoulders slumped, but without complaint.

Was she being a brat? Really, what *did* she have to complain about? Second-rate food and a cold bed? Hadn't she asked for that when she'd disobeyed Thomas and snuck onto the train?

Jonah and Britt didn't ask for any of this. They'd been slaves their whole lives, whipped like workhorses. Spent the only two days of freedom they'd ever known running from dogs and slave catchers who wanted to kidnap and sell them again.

I am being a brat! She closed her eyes and banged one fist on her forehead. *Stupid!* No more brat. No more whining. What happens, happens.

Deal with it, Connors.

She almost laughed. Her soccer coach had once said those very words to her. Late in a tournament the previous spring, she'd argued with a referee about a bad call and had gotten a yellow card. She'd kept complaining, though, and the referee gave her a red card and ejected her from the game. Down a player, her team had given up two goals in the final five minutes and lost the championship. She'd been so angry with that referee, blaming it all on him. But it had been *her* fault.

Deal with it, Connors.

Fine. She *could* deal with the cold, with the lack of food, with the exhausting travels. It wasn't about her. It was to help Britt and Jonah. And if she ever did get home, she could deal with her father's marriage, too. Because—duh. That wasn't about her, either.

131

She growled to herself, "Deal with it, Connors!"

* * *

Ty followed the streets back toward the river and looked down upon the Chestertown port from a hill. The concrete docks were a bustle of activity, as they had always been in Philadelphia. He spotted a dozen schooners and smaller fishing vessels. Farther along was a square-rigged clipper flying a British flag atop its mainmast. It looked skinny for its length and too large for a river, so he guessed they weren't too far from the Chesapeake Bay.

Beyond the clipper a side-wheeled steamer was tied up. The red wheel took up half the far side of the vessel. Tendrils of smoke curled from the charcoal gray smokestacks. That would be his ride north, he guessed.

He descended the hill and followed the sidewalk parallel to the waterfront. Dozens of brick-faced buildings and warehouses lined the walk. He found a shed-like office jutting from a wall of one warehouse and entered. A fat man sat behind a desk, scrawling in a ledger. Round spectacles perched on his bulbous nose and thick sideburns grew like thistles across both cheeks and hung past his jowls.

"Excuse me, sir," Ty said. "But—"

"Boy!" the man yelled over his shoulder without looking up. "Bring me the quarterly logs."

A moment later a skinny kid with sandy-blonde hair scurried from the back room cradling two black books in long, gangly arms. He, too, ignored Ty, dropping the books onto the man's desk. "Here you go, Mr. Jamison."

The man grabbed the first book, glanced at the cover, and a flush mottled his quivering cheeks. "Not *this* quarter's, you idiot! *Last* quarter's." He jettisoned the book to the corner. "I swear you're useless as a feathered paperweight."

"Sorry, Mr. Jamison." The boy retrieved the book and scurried to the back room.

"Excuse me, sir," Ty said again. "Can you—"

"I've no need for more inept boys," the man interrupted, still without looking up. "Leave the way you came in."

"I'm not looking for a job, sir. Just passage north."

"Do I look like a ferry captain, you idiot?"

"No, sir, but—"

"Then get out before I have you horse-whipped." He picked up an apple from his desk and flung it. Ty ducked and the apple splattered on the wall. The man grunted and picked up a stone paperweight.

"I'm going, I'm going." Ty scurried to the door, yanked it open, and ran face-first into a broad chest. Ty stumbled back. It felt as if he'd hit a brick wall. He looked up to see the man could've passed for one. He was huge as a story-book ogre. His almond-shaped eyes were a dull gray and his mouth hung open.

"I'm sorry," Ty said, feeling his aching nose. He blinked away the tears forming in his eyes. "I—I didn't see you."

The big man grunted.

"No, the fault lies with my companion, young man. Not you," said another man, who'd stepped up beside the ogre. This one was a scarecrow, tall and skinny, with a long, jutting nose and pointy chin. He took off his hat and gave a slight bow. "We beg *your* pardon."

"No problem," Ty said. "Well, uh—have a good day."

He turned to leave, but the scarecrow man gripped his arm.

"Where are you off to so quickly, young man?"

Ty looked down at the hand on his arm. The man had a firm grip. Not tight enough yet to hurt, but enough to say he *could* hurt Ty if he wanted.

"Just looking for work loading and unloading is all," Ty said.

"Ahh, an industrious youth." The man's smile was warm, but his eyes were dark and calculating. "Well, don't let us hold you back from an honest day's work. Good luck, lad." He let go of Ty's arm and patted it.

"Thank you, sir." Ty continued down the walk. Pausing to cross a street, he glanced back. The two men were coming down the walk this way as well. An uneasy feeling made his skin crawl.

Oh, stop being paranoid, he thought, shaking his head.

Farther down the pier was the ticket office for the steamer. He got in line, counting five people ahead. The brass bell over the door rung a few times as more entered. After about ten minutes, he reached the counter. The clerk was a middle-aged man with a bushy mustache.

"May I help you, lad?"

"Um, where is the steamer going?"

"Shoving off for Annapolis in thirty minutes. Be another this afternoon, steaming north to Elkton."

The bell over the door jingled again. Ty glanced back and saw the ogre and scarecrow enter the ticket office. It couldn't be a coincidence. They were following him. But why?

"So what'll it be, lad?" the clerk asked, drumming his finger on the wooden counter, glancing around Ty at the next customer.

"Um—" He glanced back again. They couldn't know who he was, could they? He wasn't—*the jailhouse!* They must have followed him. But why didn't they just arrest him? Then it dawned on him. They must be hoping he'd lead them to Kristi and the others.

The clerk frowned. "If you're not buying a ticket, young man, I'll have to ask you to—"

"Annapolis," Ty blurted, loud enough for everyone to hear. "One-way ticket to Annapolis."

"One dollar."

Ty handed over Thomas's cash and took the ticket. Then he lowered his head and left, passing by the ogre and scarecrow without looking up. As soon as the door closed behind him, he ran across the street toward a throng of people gathered on the pier. He zigzagged through the crowd and hid behind an empty booth. He waited, watching the door of the ticket office. The men emerged a few minutes later. They stopped on the wooden walk and scanned the pier. The scarecrow said something and pointed left. They split up. The ogre walked around the crowd of people, the scarecrow went straight through.

So they *were* following him. He needed to play this just right, then. If they discovered he was on to them, they could arrest him and he'd never get help for Kristi. He stepped away from the booth, into plain sight. From the corner of one eye, he saw the scarecrow turn his head and motion to the other. Ty walked toward the steamer as if on a Sunday stroll, but his heart beat like a bongo-player's wild solo.

A whistle atop the steamer blew high and long. Black smoke from the stacks thickened. Ty waited in a line, handed his ticket to a man at the end, and climbed the gangway and the stairs to the deck and went toward the aft. There, he leaned against the railing and looked down. The pier lay about ten feet down with a gap of about a foot between it and the boat, which pitched on small waves. Suddenly the broad expanse of planks below looked very narrow.

He saw the two men board the ship. After a couple minutes, they showed again on the deck, but toward the fore.

Good. Get a good look at me.

The whistle blew three short blasts. Two hands hauled the gangway aboard. The steamer listed and started swinging away from the pier, bow first.

Ty jumped onto the railing, balanced there a moment, then sat and hung his legs over. The gap between the boat and the pier widened a couple feet. He took a deep breath and leapt. A woman's shrill scream pierced the air. His feet hit hard and he rolled, banging one knee. Grimacing, he rolled onto his back and looked up. The steamer was steadily pulling away, the gap now ten feet, now fifteen.

A small crowd gathered at the rail. Ty saw the ogre and scarecrow push through and lean over. He could actually make out the curses on the smaller man's lips.

Ty stood and grinned, despite the throbbing knee, giving salute to the departing boat. Then he disappeared into the crowd on the pier.

THIRTEEN

Kristi turned over on the cool dirt floor of the root cellar. All around her rose the even, sleeping breaths of the others. Groaning, she pulled a scratchy blanket over her head and tried to go back to sleep. But in the pitch black, the cellar could've been a coffin.

Deal with it!

She'd seen Jonah watching as they'd settled in, as if waiting for her to complain. Instead she'd bitten her lip and swallowed her complaints back. No whining.

They were hidden below the cellar at another Quaker's house, a friend of Johann's named Isaac.

She was touched by the help these men had provided, the danger they were putting themselves into with no reward. Johann had taken them into his home even while the patrollers were in hot pursuit. He'd fed and clothed them, then delivered them safely here. Now this man Isaac was sheltering them. He'd agreed to smuggle them into Delaware in his wagon. To others who would help them get north.

These two Quakers were breaking the law for strangers. They could be arrested and lose everything for a wayfaring band of runaways neither had ever met before.

She'd understood the dangers Thomas invited when he'd agreed to help Jonah and Britt. He helped because *she* needed it. She understood Bo's selflessness as well. He'd been a slave and Thomas had helped him, and he was paying it forward.

Of course she'd studied the Underground Railroad in school. Her history book seemed full of stories about Harriet Tubman and other black conductors. But she'd never considered the help Tubman would've needed from white people as well. Her teachers had never mentioned the part Quakers had played hiding slaves, moving them north. Tubman and the others couldn't have delivered so many runaways if it hadn't been for the Quakers' help.

She yawned, overcome by sudden warming pride. She was following in the footsteps of the woman called Moses. Exhaustion won, and she finally slept.

The hours of rest ticked off like mere minutes, though. All too soon, the door at the top of the stairs scraped open. Kristi flinched and blinked against the wedge of bright morning light that fell on her face. Booted feet clomped down the steps until Isaac emerged, carrying an oil lamp. His clothes were the same style of dark pants and bloused white shirt Johann had been wearing. He had the same chin-concealing beard and shaved upper lip, though Isaac's was thicker and streaked with gray.

"It is time," he said, passing around small loaves of brown bread and strips of dried beef for each of them.

Kristi got up with the others and stretched. As she moved about and the initial grogginess wore off, she found she was not as weary as she'd thought. Her neck was stiff from sleeping on the ground with no pillow, but her legs didn't ache as they had during the previous days. Her whole body felt stronger.

I can actually do this, she thought, smiling.

"So we get to ride in the wagon today, right?" That would be a treat. By now, her blisters had calluses.

Isaac nodded. "But there are Christian Wolves about. The roads aren't safe to travel on foot, even at night. I shall take you into Delaware. There others will guide you north."

Kristi frowned. "Christian Wolves? Who—"

"Code name for slave catchers," Bo said. "That man Mackey and his friends."

At the mention of the name, Britt stiffened. He made no sound, but grabbed Jonah's arm and looked up with eyes that screamed alarm. Jonah put a hand on Britt's and squeezed. "It'll be all right."

Isaac nodded. "There are other underground passengers out as well. And other Wolves. It shall not be an easy road."

"So what makes us safer in a wagon?" Kristi asked.

"I'll show you." Isaac smiled. "Come."

She followed him up the stairs, marveling at the difference in temperature just a few feet of earth made. The cellar had been far from balmy, but, with a blanket, warm enough to sleep without shivering. Yet up top, out in the open air, her breath puffed out in great white clouds. Flaky frost glazed the grass and crunched under foot. They might've frozen if they'd spent another night outside.

Isaac led them to a wagon hitched behind two draft horses. The bed was already packed with full potato sacks and split logs, leaving no room for passengers.

Kristi's brow knitted. "Where do we ride?"

Isaac reached down and removed a board, a false floor concealing the bottom of the wagon bed. About a foot high, it ran the length and width of the bed.

"You shan't be discovered," he said.

She flashed back to the refrigerator and the ill-fated game of hide-n-seek. "No, no. What if it collapses?"

"There's no danger of collapse," Isaac said.

She shook her head, already having trouble pulling a full breath. "But—but, we won't be able to breathe."

"I've transported others by the same method. You have nothing to fear."

"But—But—"

Jonah rolled his eyes. "You'd prefer a padded coach seat?" *White man's pet* was practically scrolling across his face.

Her cheeks burned. "Shut-up, Jonah!" He couldn't understand, even if she tried to explain.

"We've no choice," Bo said. "It's the safest way."

She looked from face to face, searching for an ally. Jonah's lip curled with disgust. Even Bo looked annoyed. But Britt—pity in his dark eyes? The boy who was afraid of his own shadow felt sorry for *her*?

"I—I—" She threw up her hands. "Fine!"

Bo climbed in first, followed by Jonah, then Britt. Kristi stood behind the wagon, tried to stop her hands from shaking as they gripped the plank.

Deal with it, Connors!

She slid in feet first, farther, farther, until she'd drawn her head into the compartment. It smelled of must and mildew. The top was so close it seemed to press down on her, not letting her fill her lungs.

Isaac fit the board over the opening. Kristi closed her eyes. Bright stars flashed behind her lids. She clawed at the boards underneath her, breathing in short, choppy bursts.

"I—I can't breath!"

She reached up, about to shove the board away, but a hand caught hers and held on.

"S'all right," said a breathy child's voice in her ear. "Ain' nothin' gonna happen."

"Who is—*Britt*?"

He squeezed her hand tighter. "Think o' some place else," he whispered. "That what Jonah tell me when I'm scart."

"But I—I thought you didn't talk to anyone but Jonah."

"I don't." She couldn't see his face, but she felt sure the boy was smiling.

She tried to picture the huge auditorium back at her school. No good. Then a wide-open meadow—yes, that helped a little. A winding creek gurgling over stones. Knee-high grasses, dotted with wildflowers, swaying with the breeze. She could almost hear birds chirping, smell the wildflowers, feel the cool creek water splashing her feet. After a minute, the pounding in her head lessened, then stopped.

The wagon lurched forward, bumping along the unpaved road.

I can do this!

"Th—thank you, Britt."

He squeezed her hand, but didn't speak again.

* * *

An hour or so into the trip, the wagon jerked to a stop. Kristi heard the clop-clop of hooves. Then Isaac's voice, muffled by the boards.

"Good day to you."

"We're searching for runaways. Four of 'em," a deep, gruff voice snapped. "A man, two boys, and a girl."

"I've seen none of that description this morn," Isaac said.

"You won't mind us searchin' your wagon, then," said another voice, higher pitched, scratchy. *Mackey!* "They're the very devil at hidin' away."

Britt must've recognized it, too. He started trembling. His breaths came faster. Seconds later, Kristi caught the unmistakable odor of urine.

She grasped his hand and squeezed. "It's all right," she whispered. "He can't find us in here."

"As it happens, I do mind." Isaac answered, voice even, matter-of-fact. "I've done nothing wrong. You have no cause to search my property."

"Well, as it happens, I *do* have cause," Mackey sneered. A paper rustled. "This-here's a signed warrant, giving us leave to search wherever we please. The runaways burnt down an inn. The judge wants to see 'em hanged in Chestertown."

Britt whimpered. Kristi covered his mouth. "Shhhh!"

"I'm sorry, gentlemen, but we crossed the Delaware border five miles back. Warrants issued by Maryland county judges have no power over state lines."

Mackey's voice rose. "But the Fugitive Slave Law says—"

"I've read the Bloodhound Act," Isaac interrupted. "It says nothing of subjecting citizens to illegal search without due cause. But I haven't the time to debate. If it will put me on my way more quickly, you are free to look through my wagon. But be quick. I've already tarried too long."

"Then why deny us in the first place?"

"Perhaps only to show I know my rights." Isaac's voice was still calm. "Or, perhaps, to delay you and give the children of God you hunt a better chance of escaping to freedom."

"Empty it," Mackey growled.

Boots thumped on the ground. The wagon jostled as men climbed aboard. She heard the contents being taken up and thrown over the side. After a couple minutes, one of the men on the wagon called out, "Nothin' but taters and kindlin' wood."

"Well, *Friend*," Mackey snorted. "Now you got the *right* to reload and be on your way."

"Indeed. But I shall make a complaint to Judge Sampson of the county office in Chestertown," Isaac said. "What is your name?"

Mackey laughed. "Horace Humphries. Tell Sampson I told you to go sit on a billy goat."

The other men laughed. Finally Kristi heard them ride off.

"They are gone," Isaac called softly.

"We're safe!" she said, stroking Britt's arm.

He slumped against her shoulder and sobbed.

* * *

Ty crouched at the bow of the ferry, away from the lanterns and, hopefully, the notice of the other passengers. He peered between the railings, scanning the wharf as the ferry docked at Elkton. Darkness had settled and lanterns lit the docks with flickering globes, making it hard to distinguish features. Still, he didn't spot Ogre or Scarecrow. No way they could've made it to Elkton ahead of him. But there could be others.

He looked for groups of men who might be watching the boat. For dim shapes lurking in the shadows. But the upturned faces were sparse, many of them family groups, and none jumped out at him.

When the boat was tied up and the gangway lowered, Ty weaved into the midst of the disembarking passengers. Once on the pier, he moved into the shadows beside an empty ticket booth and did some lurking of his own. Nobody seemed to be watching. Still, he walked away from the wharf, checking behind him now and then. He ducked through stinking alleyways and down empty streets. After half an hour, he found the train station, the gated window to the ticket office dark and shuttered.

"Oh, grand," he muttered, rattling the lock. "Just grand!" He had money, could hire a room for the night, sit next to a fire, sleep in a bed, then catch a train in the morning. How tired he was! When had he last slept? He'd spent the previous night up a tree, and had dozed fitfully on the ferry. But good, long hearty sleep seemed only a distant memory.

Still, going to an inn alone could bring questions he didn't want to answer.

He found a bench beneath a leafless oak behind the station, but the wind was brisk, the air frigid, too cold without a blanket. He thought of Kristi. What was she doing? Where was she sleeping? There would be no inns welcoming her. No hot food or warm fires.

Resigned, he lay back on the hard bench, pulled his arms through his sleeves and wrapped them around his body. It was so cold. Surely he wouldn't sleep a wink.

But he soon fell senseless into a broken sleep, dreaming of polar bears and ice caps.

* * *

Kristi eased from the tight compartment. She more or less tumbled over the side and staggered against the wagon, trying to work some feeling back into her legs. Then stretched her arms and twisted until her spine popped like a string of firecrackers.

The wagon was stopped before tall iron gates with spear-head tips set between concrete walls too high to see over. Ominous, curvy shapes stood sentry atop the walls on either side of the gate, outlined against the night sky. The moon slid out for a moment from under a blanket of clouds, and she saw the shapes were statues. Concrete cherubs, naked babies with carved ringlets and stubby wings. An icy shiver ran up the back of her neck.

After the other three climbed out, Isaac replaced the board. "You must tread softly, now."

Kristi frowned. "Where are we?"

"A graveyard in Middletown. It's another twenty miles to Wilmington. Others shall see you safely the rest of the way. Follow the path." He pointed through the iron gates. "You will find the party in question at the chapel."

A narrow, graveled path started at the gates, wound among the gravestones, and disappeared into the dark. Kristi shuddered.

"But aren't you coming with us?"

"Nay," Isaac said. "The less I see now, the safer you shall be later."

Bo and Jonah pushed the iron gate. Its hinges gave a low, gloomy creak as it swung open. Kristi took Isaac's hand.

"Thank you!" she said. "Thanks for everything."

He nodded. "Do not tarry. Godspeed."

Kristi followed the others through the gate. The moon cast long, eerie shadows among the gravestones, then disappeared behind another cloud. They stuck close, following the curving path up a hill. Every now and then gloomy marble mausoleums with intricate carvings seemed to jump out of the dark.

When they reached the top of the hill the moon made another brief appearance. A building sat down the slope. Large, darkened windows were set into the wall facing them. A cross jutted into the sky above it. Kristi strained her eyes and ears, but sensed no movement in or around the chapel. Were they too late? Maybe the escape party had come and gone. Would they have to make their way north alone?

She moved past the others and started down the hill.

"Stay," Bo hissed.

She ignored him, hurrying toward the chapel. Maybe the others Isaac told them about hadn't gotten too far yet and they could catch up. She rounded a corner of the chapel and something slammed into her stomach, knocking the wind from her. She crumpled to her knees. A black shape suddenly loomed overhead. Cold metal pressed against her temple.

"Move a muscle and you be seein' through a hole in da side o' yoah head."

FOURTEEN

The Wilmington train station was a bustle of activity, just as Ty had hoped.

He pressed himself into the stream of passengers exiting the train, alert for less-than-friendly faces. There were well-dressed men in waist coats and top hats, women with lacy shawls, bonnets, and button up boots, boys in suits with little cravats and caps, and girls in capes with puffed out skirts and hats that made them look dollish. But everyone seemed to be about his or her own business. No one paid any attention to him.

He followed the cobblestone street past two taverns, then ducked between a shop and a warehouse and down an alleyway that smelled of rotten eggs and horse manure. He doubled back on his route a few times to make sure no one followed him.

Finally satisfied that he wasn't being tailed, he stepped back onto an open street and scanned the businesses lining it. There was a general store, a smith, and another tavern, but no hardware stores.

How was he going to find Mr. Garrett? He didn't have a clue where to start.

He turned up a brick road, passing beneath signs marking tailor's and cobbler's shops. A red-headed boy with a canvas satchel hanging from his shoulders appeared from the door of a law office and stepped onto the street. The boy held a newspaper in one hand and was walking toward Ty.

"Excuse me." Ty held up a hand to stop him. "I'm trying to find a man named Thomas Garrett. Could you tell me where I could find his hardware shop?"

The boy, who stopped and eyed him for a moment, looked to be ten or eleven with freckles dotting his cheeks and nose. "What's it worth, then?"

Ty shrugged. "A copper penny, I guess."

The boy looked disgusted. "*Two* coppers."

"Done." Ty dug the two coins from his pocket and held out his hand.

"Meant ta say *five*," the boy blurted, taking a step back.

Ty closed his fist on the coins. "Wait a minute. You said two, mate."

"Price went up." The boy shrugged. "Mr. Garrett's a hard man to find."

"Fine," Ty sighed. "But that's all." He dug the additional coins out.

The boy grinned and swiped them up. "Garrett's hardware's on the waterfront. Everybody knows *that*."

"Thanks," Ty said wryly, thinking—*yeah, everybody but me.* "How do I get there?"

The boy raised an eyebrow and smirked. "Depends on how much more money you got to spend." He held out a hand again.

Ty rolled his eyes and pushed past. "Forget it. I'll find it myself."

The boy laughed. "Good luck!"

Ty crossed toward a busier street, stepping aside to avoid being run down by a mule-drawn cart, then crossed to a grocer's shop. He passed a butcher, smelling fresh meat, salted ham, and other spices. His stomach grumbled.

Ahead he saw a courthouse with stone pillars and long concrete steps. Next to it stood a smaller clapboard building with bars over the windows.

"Uh-oh," he muttered and avoided these, crossing a street. Finally he saw the river ahead.

The waterfront was lined with more shops and taverns. Two blocks farther down he found a small storefront with wide windows. The sign above the door read *Garrett's Iron and Hardware*.

Ty stepped inside and found an open floor-space that smelled musty, almost metallic. Two squared wooden pillars stood in the center and beams hung overhead. Axes, saws, and hammers covered the walls and hung from the rafters. A balding man with round glasses and a mustache stood behind a counter, bent over a ledger.

"Excuse me, sir." Ty cleared his throat. "I'm looking for Mr. Garrett."

The man didn't look up from doing his books. "Don't got no job for you, boy."

"I'm not looking for work," Ty said. "I just need to see Thomas Garrett."

The man sighed, let his pencil drop, and looked up as if bored. "Mr. Garrett's a busy man. Got no time for shiftless rascals and lay-abouts."

"Please," Ty said. "I need his help. My friends are in trouble."

The man planted both hands on the countertop and scowled. "I told you. Mr. Garrett's busy. Move along now, sonny."

"No!" Ty crossed his arms. "I'm *not* leaving until I see him."

The man's eyebrows raised. He picked up a long, thin wooden stick and rounded the counter. "You lookin' for a thrashin', boy."

Ty lifted his chin. "No, just for Mr. Garrett. If you'd tell him that Thomas Jordan is—"

The man raised the stick high. "I warned you—"

"Hold, Samuel," interrupted another voice. The clerk's hand froze in midair. He looked back over one shoulder. Ty followed his gaze and saw an old man standing before an open door in the back of the shop. His hair was snow white, wild and unkempt, face etched with wrinkles. He wore a black suit and a loose cravat. "I'm Thomas Garrett, son. What do you want with me?"

Ty pushed past the clerk. "Mr. Garrett, please listen. Thomas Jordan sent me. He's in trouble."

Garrett's eyebrows descended in a bushy V. "Thom? What kind of trouble?"

"He was arrested. He's in a jail in Chestertown. They said he stole slaves, burnt down an inn, and killed the innkeeper. I swear it's all bloody lies! But they might hang him."

"I see. Was Dr. Jordan caught in the company of the runaways?"

"They're *not* runaways," Ty said. "I mean, not really. Thomas bought and paid for them. He meant to free them. But some slave catchers burned their papers and said Thomas stole the boys. Then the sheriff arrested him. Bo got himself and the others away. Thomas thinks they're coming here."

Garrett turned to the clerk, who had gone back to the counter. "Samuel, call on Mr. Johnston. Have him send a telegram to Mr. Lewis in Chestertown. He will see to Dr. Jordan."

"Yes, sir," the clerk said and left the shop.

"Who are Mr. Johnson and Mr. Lewis?" Ty asked.

"Johnson's my lawyer and Lewis is an associate of mine in Chestertown who knows the sheriff. He'll see that Thomas is released. You say Bo is bringing the others here?"

"That's what Thomas said. But there are patrollers out looking for them."

"Bo knows how to evade the Wolves," Garrett said. "It happens I'm expecting other *passengers* as well. Perhaps they shall assist each other."

Ty gasped. "There's more coming? Right now?"

Garrett nodded. "Yes, and they'll be led by a most accomplished conductor."

* * *

"Move an' I'll shoot you, girl," the dark shape said, pressing the gun barrel into Kristi's temple. "Wha'dyou want here?"

"Please don't shoot," Kristi cried. "Isaac sent us. We need help."

"*Us?*" The gunman stepped back, keeping the gun trained on Kristi. "Who else is along?" The moon made another brief appearance and shone pale light on the assailant. Kristi's mouth dropped open. The gunman was a gun*woman*! Her dark eyes shined with anger.

"You hear me, girl?" the woman prodded. "Betta speak up right quick, den. How many?"

"F—four," Kristi said. "Just four."

The woman swore colorfully as a sailor, then shoved the gun into a rope cinched around the waist of her dark dress. "Nobody tol' me nothin' 'bout four more. How'm I s'posed to get north wit half o' Mar'lan along?" She jabbed a finger at Kristi. "You gonna get us caught!"

"Oh, no we won't," Kristi promised. "We'll be quiet as...as mice. Quieter! You won't even know we're here."

Soft footfalls approached, and a hand touched her shoulder.

"You okay?" Bo's voice asked.

She nodded. "Yes, but—"

"Hello, Harriet," Bo said. "It's been a long time."

Harriet? Kristi eyed the woman. *Not Harriet...no. Couldn't be.* This woman wasn't much taller than Kristi. Her heavy cloak and scarf made her look stocky, kind of like somebody's grandma. Not heroic. Her face was broad, but lined and hardened, making it hard to tell her age. But the eyes—they were young and full of life.

"So who's dat?" The woman squinted. "Bo? What you doin' wit all dese chil'ins?"

He sighed. "On account of Dr. Jordan. We ran into trouble with a pack of Wolves at Chestertown. So now we're headed to Wilmington."

She snorted. "'Nother one of Jordan's cock'mamie schemes?"

Bo's eyes glinted. "You could say that."

"Y'all been followed?"

"Yes, ma'am," Bo admitted.

Harriet swore. "Den dese chil'ins better not slow me down." She spun and tromped away.

Bo started to follow, but Kristi grabbed his arm.

"Harriet?" she said. "Is that—Moses? I mean, like, really *Harriet Tubman*?"

"It is." Bo nodded, his lips twitching as if he might laugh.

Kristi glanced the legend's retreating back. Her legs suddenly felt weaker than when she'd had the gun stuck to her head. *Holy cow!*

She grabbed Jonah's arm as he passed. "You know who *that* is? It's Harriet Tubman! Really! Can you believe it? We're going on the Underground Railroad with THE Harriet Tubman!"

"Yeah." Jonah shrugged out of her grip. "So what?"

She turned to the younger boy. "Did you hear that, Britt. Harriet *Tubman*. We're as good as saved!"

Britt nodded, looking unimpressed, and followed his brother.

"Jeez!" she cried, throwing her hands up. "Doesn't anyone care? This is, like, real *history*!"

Shaking her head, she followed the others around the chapel. Harriet stopped on the other side to speak to a man and a woman leaning back, beneath the shadow of the eaves. The man, even bigger and more imposing than Bo, wore a ragged frockcoat and torn trousers, cut off below the knees. He had an arm around the shoulders of the woman, who wore a gray day gown with a white headscarf, neatly tied, kind of like a low turban. She hugged a bundle of cloth to her chest. But when Kristi looked closer, she saw a small, sleeping face snuggled there against the woman's bosom.

"We gots to get movin'," Harriet said. "Keep at chil' quiet, hear?"

"Yes'm," the woman squeaked. She sounded terrified. *Well, no wonder,* Kristi thought.

"If'n he starts to bawlin', we's in foah trouble."

"She...she's a girl, missus," the woman said. "She don't cry much."

Harriet nodded. "Good. All right. We got a long road ahead. Y'all keep quiet, lessen you wanna get caught an' dragged back south."

Harriet led the silent procession through the graveyard and out a gate at the other end. They followed a curved path through a wood and then along the bottom of a twisting ravine. The clouds thinned, then disappeared altogether. The moon bathed the woods in a clear, pale light, casting queer shadows between the leafless trees.

Kristi came up to the woman and baby.

"What's her name?" she whispered.

"Rose," the woman said softly, smiling a little, lower lip trembling. "Rose Lily."

"That's pretty. I'm Kristi."

"I'm Abigail. That's Sam." She pointed shyly to the man.

"Is he your husband?"

She shook her head. "Massa don' let none o' us house servants git married. Weren't gonna let me keep Rose, neither. Said she'd git in da way of my work. He already took two of my babies. They was jus' toddlin', so I—" Her voice caught. She took a deep breath. "But me an' Sam's gonna git married, up north. Find us a real church, a real preacher. Not jus' jump de broom. Den Sam's gonna go find my boys, bring 'em north too."

"They took away your kids?" Kristi said, too loud, then bit her lip. She flashed back to the whining she'd done about her dad getting remarried like it was the end of the world. Kristi would've laughed out loud how childish that would sound to escaping slaves with real worries, but she didn't want Abigail to think she was mocking her, as Jonah had, earlier. "Ms. Tubman will get us north safely, I know it," she said. "And my friend Thomas will help get your boys back. He's a good man. He's done it before."

Abigail smiled politely, but Kristi could tell she didn't put much stock in the promises of a wild-eyed, filthy, twelve-year-old runaway.

Kristi slowed and turned back to Jonah, who was close behind. She took a deep breath, whispered, "Hey, look. I—I'm sorry I have been such a brat, Jonah. Can we call a truce?"

He eyed her strangely. For a second she thought he was going to scoff and push on past.

"Thanks for pullin' Britt from that river," he said grudgingly, grimacing at the end as if the words actually hurt his mouth coming out. "Thanks for comfortin' him back in the wagon."

She shrugged and looked ahead to make sure Britt was out of earshot. "Why is he so terrified of Mackey, anyway? He goes to pieces every time that snake is even mentioned."

Jonah sighed. "Mackey always had it out for Britt, always got some sick pleasure out of tormentin' him."

"But, why?"

"Guess he's an easy target. Mackey'd come 'round the plantation from time to time. He's some relation to Massa Conwell, cousin I think. He'd get drunk with the handlers, then bet on how quick he could get Britt to wet hisself. Never took 'em long." He clenched his fists. "Once, he held Britt's head in a water trough 'til Britt stopped thrashin'. He mighta drowned him if I hadn't come along and knocked Mackey out. Got me thirty lashes, then five days without food. But Mackey ain't hurt Britt since, though he keeps on harassin' him e'ery chance he gets."

"Monster!" She spat on the ground. "We're going to get Britt away, so he never has to worry about that beast again."

Jonah nodded.

Kristi sighed. "I'm going to be tougher, too. I know it drives you crazy when I complain about sleeping outdoors and all. I'm not going to whine anymore."

"You been as tough a girl as any I've seen." Jonah admitted. "You really ain't no white man's pet."

"Thanks," she said, her skin tingling.

Hours later, as dawn broke over the low, marshy area through which they'd slogged, she wanted to eat her words. Harriet had pushed them through the countryside all night, rarely pausing for rest. When a pink glow lightened the gray sky over the trees to the west, Harriet halted, saying it was too dangerous to move through the day.

They'd stopped next to a pond with a thin layer of ice across its surface. The ground was black mud, somewhere between frozen and mush. Kristi, Bo, Jonah, and Britt sat hidden under the poky leaves of a holly tree with bright red berries. Harriet and the others were hidden in a similar tree a dozen yards away.

Icy sleet drenched the marsh. The tree kept most of the rain off, but a few trickles made their way through. One dripped maddeningly down the back of Kristi's neck. She was freezing, hungry, tired, and sore. Complaints rose on her tongue, but she looked at Jonah beside her, fast asleep, and swallowed them back. The others were asleep, too, curled up as if on a feather bed in a cushy hotel. She scooted closer to Jonah so the drips fell on the ground beside her and closed her eyes. Another icy drop plinked on her head. She chuckled ruefully; it was either that or cry. She closed her eyes and finally slept, her head on Jonah's broad shoulder.

* * *

The next night's trek went by in a blur of chilly footsoreness. They'd moved from dusk until dawn, skirting sleeping communities and avoiding farmhouses. At daybreak, they stopped in a thick glade of evergreens and stretched out, cushioned by thick pine needles. The rain had stopped, the temperature rose enough to thaw the ground. This time, Kristi'd had no trouble sleeping the day through.

Upon waking, they ate the last of the bread Isaac had packed and the hardtack Harriet had provided. Harriet said that with a good pace, they would reach a Quaker meeting by morning. There, they'd stock up for the final leg to Mr. Garrett's in Wilmington, which they should reach the following night.

That news, plus the strangely decent sleep she'd gotten, put pep in Kristi's step. Wilmington the next night, then perhaps Thomas's farm the following. Ty and Thomas would have to be there by now. They'd be so impressed. She'd set off to rescue Jonah and Britt, to save Britt from disappearing into history, and she'd have done it. Ty wouldn't believe she actually met Harriet Tubman.

The night was so dark she had to squint to keep sight of Britt's silhouette, though he was only a few steps ahead. But the moonless obscurity had pleased Harriet. She said that any Wolves in the area couldn't possibly find them if they only stayed quiet. So the little band traveled in silence, each lost in thought.

Rose Lily whimpered a few times and cried out once, a thin, kittenish wail. But Abigail was able to hush her with soft sways and gentle words in the baby's ear.

After a few hours, Harriet stopped everyone under a copse of evergreens.

"Stay here and don' make no noise," she whispered. "Dere's a bridge ahead. I'll scout it 'afore y'all come trundlin' out makin' noise."

Kristi hunkered down with the rest and Tubman went off. Rose Lily woke and whimpered softly, but Abigail quieted her.

After twenty minutes, Harriet returned.

"Dere's lanterns on da bridge," she said. It was too dark to read her face, but the anxiety in Harriet's voice was plain. "We got to swim across."

To her left, Kristi felt Britt stiffen.

"Keep that baby quiet, too," Harriet said. "Dere's Wolves about. I ken smell 'em."

"I will," Abigail said. "She won't make no noise."

"Can't take no chances." Harriet took a small vial from her bag and approached Abigail. "A couple drops will keep her sleepin'."

Abigail twisted the baby away. "You ain't givin' my baby no potions," she said. "She ain't gonna cry."

"Now don' you argue wit me, girl," Harriet said. "If'n she cries, Wolves'll be down on us like we's lambs. It ain't gone hurt none, jus' keep her sleepin'."

Abigail shot a horrified glance at Sam. He sighed, laid a big hand on her shoulder, and nodded. "It'll be safer."

The young mother futilely searched the other faces for support, then sighed. Tears rolled down her cheeks. "What's in it?"

"Belladonna in a sugar syrup." Harriet pulled a dropper from the vial and squeezed two tiny drops into Rose's mouth. The baby's face screwed up, then she licked her lips and cooed.

"Dere," Harriet said. "We gotta move, now."

She dropped the vial back into her bag and led them down a long hill. After a quarter mile, Kristi heard the gurgle and splash of moving water. They followed the river another mile or so, away from the bridge, before Harriet found the spot she wanted to cross. This river wasn't much wider than the first they'd crossed. A wall of thick-trunked trees stood on the other bank.

"Find a branch or log big 'nough to hang onto," Harriet instructed. Kristi spread out with the others and was searching the bank when she noticed Britt, hanging far back from the water's edge.

After twenty minutes, they'd found enough for each of them. Sam brought a log big enough to hold the baby.

Remembering her last trip into the river, Kristi didn't balk when Harriet told them all to take off their clothes. Besides, it was too dark for any of the others to see her.

"Keep them clothes outta da water," Harriet said. "It gets deep in the middle, so kick on across holdin' dem branches."

Sam and Abigail stepped in first. Sam kept hold of the log with the baby. Bo went next, then Jonah.

Britt stood frozen on the bank, still clothed.

"Come on, boy," Harriet said. "Jus' keep hold o' dat branch."

He backed away.

Moses frowned. Her voice hardened. "Ain't no time to turn coward. Ain't no other way, 'cept to deal with dem Wolves on da bridge."

"Come on, Britt," Kristi urged. "I won't let you go under."

He glanced at her, but shook his head.

"Don't think we's gonna leave you here, boy," Harriet warned. "You knows which way we goin'. Wolves get 'hold o' you, dey'll make you tell. Now git in dat water!"

Kristi reached for Britt's hand, but he sat abruptly on the bank, pressed his face to his knees, and moaned.

To Kristi's horror, Harriet drew out the pistol.

"Ain't leavin' me no choice." She pressed the barrel to Britt's head. "Move or die!"

FIFTEEN

S top it!" Kristi cried. "You're scaring him!"

"He oughta be scared."

The glint in Harriet's eyes said she wasn't bluffing, and meant to shoot if Britt didn't move.

No, Kristi thought. *Not when we're so close.* She dropped to her knees in front of the boy.

"Look at me, Britt." He didn't lift his head, so she reached out and forced his chin up. "If you get caught, they'll do horrible things to you. Then, you'll just...disappear. You'll never see Jonah again. You won't ever be free. The bad men are going to *kill* you."

"I—I can't." His voice was a scratchy whisper.

"You can!" Kristi said. "I won't let you drown. I *won't!*"

His wide eyes glistened. After a long moment, he took a deep breath, then nodded.

"Good. Now take off your clothes."

He hesitated, then grudgingly disrobed, shaking like a leaf in a windstorm.

"Take my hand," she said.

He eyed the outstretched hand, then finally gripped it.

"Just a little farther," Kristi coached. "Help me carry our log."

He did. But then, with his first step into the river, he froze. Kristi squeezed his hand and pulled him farther in. The icy water seemed to burn her ankles, but she ignored the pain and focused only on Britt. After a few steps, they were in to their waists, then shoulders. She put their clothes onto the log, then they hooked their arms over.

"Hang on tight," she whispered. Suddenly her feet weren't touching the mucky bottom of the river anymore. Britt breathed in hacking gasps.

"Breathe, just breathe," Kristi urged. "Help me. Kick your legs."

The far bank lay fifty yards ahead. Then forty, then thirty.

"Not much farther now. We're going to make it!"

But just then, Britt shrieked, slid off the log, and dipped beneath the surface.

Kristi shot a hand down, got hold of his arm, and yanked him back up. He thrashed, spurting water. But she kept a vise-like grip on his arm and kicked hard. Finally, one foot touched squishy muck again.

"We made it," she cried. "Put your feet down."

Britt's thrashing halted. When he straightened, his head stayed above the water. He smiled weakly.

"See, you made it," she said. "Keep moving."

Still gasping, he nodded and they pushed the log ahead. When they were waist deep, Jonah and Bo came down and helped them climb out. Kristi collapsed onto the sandy beach.

Britt lay beside her, his eyes closed tight.

"You...okay...Britt," she asked through chattering teeth. Her hands trembled as Bo helped her pull her dress back on.

He gave a small nod.

A minute later, Harriet emerged from the water. "Lord, y'all made 'nough racket to wake the dead. Any Wolves within two miles are like to've heard. We gotta move, now!"

As they moved through the trees, the feeling came back to Kristi's legs like fire crackling up a log. She listened for barking dogs or the clop-clop of hooves, but heard neither.

She caught up to Harriet. "You-uh, weren't really going to shoot Britt."

Harriet huffed. "What of it?"

"I mean, you wouldn't really, right? He's just a little boy. He's scared."

"We's all scared, girl. It's a scary business. But people's lives depend on me—not jus' his. And if I can make a boy more scared of me than anythin' else, he'll keep movin'."

"Then you *weren't* going to shoot."

Harriet chuckled. "I fire that gun, ev'ry Wolf in the county come swoopin' down on us."

Kristi sighed with relief and she fell back, watching the legend of the Underground Railroad walk away. Pride filled her chest. The woman really *was* Moses to her people.

A few hours later, they emerged from the trees into an empty field. A small farmhouse sat at the far end. The house was dark, but for a single lantern hanging on the porch.

Harriet pointed. "Dat means it's safe. Come on."

They all approached the house warily, but Harriet went right up to the front door and banged with one fist.

A minute later, the soft orange glow of a candle passed by the downstairs window and the door swung open. A young man in a striped nightshirt stood holding the candle. Like the other Quakers, he wore a beard, but no mustache. He looked out upon Harriet and smiled.

"I'd hoped you would arrive tonight," he said in greeting. "Please, come in from the cold."

They all filed into a small kitchen. The stone hearth had burned down to glowing coals, but it was still blessedly warm. Kristi collapsed into a ladder-backed chair.

"Dere may be Wolves on our tail, Eli," Harriet said.

The man frowned. "I can hide some, but the hidden room won't hold all of you. I'll take the others on to the next house." He left the room.

Harriet nodded and turned to Bo. "The four o' you stay here. Meet me at the foot of the bridge to Wilmington at midnight. You know it?"

Bo nodded.

When Eli returned, he wore a white shirt and dark wool trousers. A petite woman carrying a toddler followed him in. She wore a flannel night-dress and had a pretty, heart-shaped face, though her eyes were swollen from sleep. Her straight black hair hung in a long braid to the middle of her back. The chubby child struggled to get down, grunting. She set him on the floor. He wobbled for an instant, then toddled toward Kristi. He grabbed the seat of her chair and looked up.

She leaned forward and touched his springy brown curls. "Hello. What's your name?"

He stared, open mouthed, his deep, blue eyes wide with amazement.

"That's Nathan," the woman said, smiling. "He just *has* to greet all our visitors."

· "Hi, Na-than," Kristi said in a sing-song voice. She took one pudgy hand and helped him steady himself. "I'm Kristi." She patted her chest. "Kri-sti. Kristi."

The boy's mouth twitched, then widened in a grin. "Ki-Ki."

"Close enough." She laughed.

Bo turned to Eli. "Will you send word to Mr. Garrett?"

"I will." Eli turned to his wife. "Feed our weary friends, Mary. Then hide these four away. I'll not return tonight."

"Be safe, husband."

Eli bent to the little boy. "Obey thy mother, Nathan," he said, then kissed the boy's forehead.

Nathan giggled and grabbed Kristi's hand with fat fingers.

"We must go," Eli told Harriet. "We've only a few miles to the next station, but we must arrive before first light."

Abigail, Sam, and the baby left the house, followed by Eli. Harriet stopped at the open door and turned back. "Midnight," she said again. "Not a minute later."

Then she slipped away into the night.

They ate warm bread and stew in silence, then Mary pushed the table aside and pulled up the corner of the colorful rag rug beneath it. A hidden trap door had been cut into the floor.

"It's a dugout. Down you go," the Quaker woman said.

Kristi peered down into the dark and shuddered. Rats? Spiders? A door that doesn't open from the inside...

Deal with it, Connors!

She took a deep breath and climbed down the ladder first. The dugout felt damp and smelled earthy, but it was fairly warm. She found a thick, wool blanket spread across the dirt floor and lay down. She closed her eyes, trying not to think about the dark, cramped space. Bo and Britt snuggled against each shoulder, which was strangely comforting.

As Mary pushed the door closed, Kristi felt sure she wouldn't be able to sleep, but nodded off within minutes, nonetheless.

And, after what felt like only moments again, she woke with a start. Somewhere outside dogs were yelping. She sat straight up. The yips and barks got louder. She looked down at Bo. His eyes were open, staring at the ceiling.

"You hear that?" she whispered.

He blinked and nodded. A second later, the house shook from heavy pounding, probably a fist on the front door. Dust sprinkled through the boards.

Mary's light footsteps crossed the floor. "Yes?" Kristi heard her say. She sounded so...calm.

"Is this the home of Elijah Worrel?" a deep voice growled.

"Yes, but my husband is away. If you would call again, on the morrow, he'll—"

"We'll not wait," the man interrupted. Kristi heard shuffling feet, then heavy boot treads across the floor above. "We're after runaways. I'm told this is a known haven."

"That is a lie!" Mary said firmly. "I'd thank you to leave here at once. My husband is a respectable farm—"

"Your respectable husband can kiss an ape, woman," the man said. "Where y'all hiding' 'em."

Kristi crept up the ladder and put her ear to the trap door. The footsteps spread through the house. She heard furniture move and objects clunk to the floor.

"Ki-Ki," Nathan called. Light feet padded just over her head.

Kristi's heart jumped into her throat. She pictured him bending over the rug and trap door. *No, no, go away!*

"Ki-Ki, Ki-Ki, Ki-Ki," Nathan sang, jumping up and down.

Mary must have scooped him up and carried him from the room because his calls for Ki-Ki faded away.

Finally, after minutes that felt like hours, one of the men swore.

"Ain't no one here."

The heavy boots stomped back through the kitchen.

"And who will clean this mess?" Mary spat.

One of the men laughed. "Mayhap *Mr. Respectable Farmer* will clean it for you."

"Just leave," Mary said.

The men left and Mary slammed the door. Kristi melted down the ladder, laid back, and tried to calm her racing heart.

Hours later, she heard the table scrape across the floor. A hinge creaked through the dark, but she couldn't see anything.

"It's time," Mary whispered through the opening.

Kristi and the others climbed the ladder into the dark kitchen.

"There's a man at the end of the lane," Mary said. "He's been watching the house all day. You must go out the back window."

She led them through the bedroom. Nathan was sleeping in a crib next to a bed with four turned posts. Mary held a finger to her lips, opened the window, and pointed.

Kristi snuck one last look at the little boy, mouthed *thank you* to Mary, and climbed out into the frigid night. When all four were through, Bo led them toward a wooded slope. They stopped there and looked back. No movement in the dark. Bo waved and they moved through the trees.

They avoided the few other farmhouses, staying in the shadows or in the trees whenever possible. After an hour, Kristi heard moving water. Britt must've, too, for he stiffened beside her.

"Don't worry," she said. "We get to cross over on a bridge this time."

They followed the winding riverbank for a few miles, staying off the main road. Finally she spotted dark spires against the sky in the distance. As they approached, she saw it was a bridge. But, unlike the last bridge they were meant to cross, there were no lanterns on this one. The wooden bridge spanned what looked to be five hundred feet across.

Kristi heard the water moving swiftly below. She shivered, glad they wouldn't be trying to swim across *this* one.

"Where's Harriet?" she asked.

"Don't know," Bo said. "She should be here."

"Maybe she left without us. Should we cross?"

He shook his head. "No. We'll wait a spell. She'll be along."

They moved to sit under the bridge. The bank fell away after ten feet or so, giving them room to stay out of sight.

"Where is she?" Kristi asked again, a little later.

Bo didn't answer.

After about ten minutes, Kristi heard hoof-beats and the grinding of wheels spanning the bridge.

"Get down," Bo growled.

They flattened to the ground.

The wagon rattled on overhead, then was muffled on the dirt road. Kristi held her breath and prayed for the wagon to keep moving.

But the wagon stopped. She listened for feet to hit the ground. Escape was *so* close she could taste it.

They'd find Thomas's friend on the other side of that bridge. Jonah and Britt would be safe. She'd have done a great thing.

But the wagon sent cold shivers across her shoulders. It meant trouble. She just knew it. But where could they run? Swim across the river? No. They were trapped.

The same look of fear washed over even Bo's face.

She looked at Jonah and Britt with a bitter taste on her tongue.

Mimi's ancestor tree flashed into her thoughts, the yellowed parchment that had brought her back here, to 1858. She'd had no time to consider all the consequences when Mackey had ambushed them at the inn, nor when they raced across the frozen river to escape the bloodhounds.

But now, safety seemingly within reach, she let her mind run forward to the dark future that would be spawned if the boys were caught. Britt had disappeared from history once before, so the ripples through time from his capture would be minute. But *Jonah* had escaped. He'd married and had a family—*Kristi's* family. His sons and grandsons had been soldiers, bankers, lawyers. If he didn't get away, if he disappeared now, like Britt had, what would happen to her family? Would she even be born?

"Give me the time machine," she whispered to Bo. She didn't have a choice anymore. They *couldn't* get caught. She'd flash them all out of there. Not to her time, that would be too far. But maybe she'd take them ten years ahead, after the Civil War, when there'd be no more slave catchers. Who knows what that would mean about Jonah meeting his future wife and what that would do to Kristi's family, but it was their only chance.

Bo handed the rod over and Kristi typed *1868*. She took a deep breath, started to bend it into the required halo—

"Do you see anyone?" a deep voice called.

"No," answered a higher voice, the voice of a *boy*. "No one."

She shook her head. *No. My ears are playing tricks. Hearing what they want to hear.*

"Could they have crossed already?" the boy asked.

Hands trembling, she straightened the rod again and ducked out from under the wooden beams, pulling away as Bo tried to grab her.

"Ty?" she yelled. "*Ty*! We're here!"

"Kristi!" came his voice in return. Now she heard boot heels hit the ground.

She ran forward and jumped on him. They collapsed in a heap, hugging and laughing.

"You're here!" Kristi cried. "I knew you'd come!"

"Yeah?" Ty said, standing again and helping her to her feet. "Well, I knew you'd make it. That they wouldn't catch you. Where are the others?"

Bo, Jonah, and Britt emerged from under the bridge. Bo grinned as he shook Ty's hand.

"This is Samuel." Ty pointed to the driver atop the wagon. "He works for Mr. Garrett."

The man nodded. "We must go," he said. "No time to tarry."

"We can't leave yet," Kristi said. "There are others still coming." She turned to Ty. "You're not going to believe it. *Harriet Tubman*. We've been traveling with Harriet Tubman. Isn't that awesome!"

But Ty's face fell. "Yes, I know," he said. "But she's been caught. Word just got to Mr. Garrett. That's why he sent us after you."

"*Caught?*" Kristi cried. "But—how?"

"Patrollers found her safe house a few hours ago."

Kristi shook her head. "But that can't happen," she whispered. "She's—she's Moses. She's never—she's not supposed to be caught."

The safe house. Harriet was supposed to have stayed at Eli's house, safely hidden in the basement. But with Kristi and the others, there were too many, so she'd gone to *another* safe house. Her stomach wrenched. One that wasn't safe enough.

"We must go," Samuel repeated. "Mr. Garrett is waiting."

Kristi's feet wouldn't move. "No. I'm going back for Harriet."

Ty's eyes gleamed when they met hers and he nodded. "Right, then. I'm going with you."

"That is sheer folly!" Samuel protested. "You'll never find her. Let Mr. Garrett—"

"They'll take Harriet by river," Bo interrupted. "It's the fastest way out of Delaware."

"But there are Wolves about," Samuel said.

Bo shook his head. "They won't be thinking about us with a prize like Harriet. They get her on a boat, she'll be gone for good. But we may be able to catch up. If we leave now."

Kristi's jaw dropped. "You mean—you're not going to try to stop us?"

Bo grinned. "I've seen how well that works. Besides, I told Thomas I'd take care of you and I mean to see it through."

Kristi jumped up and hugged him. "Thank you!"

Jonah stepped up. "I'm comin' too."

Kristi shook her head. "Thanks, Jonah. But you have to get Britt to Mr. Garrett now. He needs you."

Jonah opened his mouth to argue, but Britt grabbed his arm.

"I—I'm going, too."

"Are you kidding me?" Kristi threw her hands up in the air. "This is too dangerous for the two of you—"

"Don't you tell me about danger," Jonah said, his jaw jutting. "You ain't keepin' us outta this."

Kristi looked from face to face, waiting for someone to agree with her and take it on. When no one did, she sighed.

"Ok, then let's go get her."

SIXTEEN

The rescue party stalked along the river's bank in determined silence. It never once occurred to Kristi to complain of the cold, or the long miles back *toward* the danger from which they'd just escaped.

She looked at Ty, who hadn't been more than a few feet from her shoulder since they'd reunited at the bridge. She'd missed him, more than she'd realized. They were a team. She couldn't help thinking that, with him by her side, her trip along the Underground would have been different. Easier, even.

She grinned and punched his shoulder. "Hey, aren't you supposed to talk me out crazy stuff like this?"

He rubbed his arm. "Things like what?"

"Oh, I don't know. Hunting slave catchers with a band of runaways and a puny white kid."

He shrugged. "As if I've ever been able to talk you out of *any* of your barmy schemes."

"You never did tell me what *barmy* means. Is it a genius, or a beautiful lady, or both?"

He laughed. "That's it *exactly*. Though, come to think of it, *arse over shoulders* might be more fitting."

She hit him again.

After nearly two hours, Bo stopped and waved everyone down.

Kristi crouched and elbow-crawled to Bo's side. "What is it?" she whispered.

"There's a fire ahead, a big one."

She followed his pointing finger and spied an orange glow between the trees in the distance. "Do you think it's them?"

"Don't know." Bo turned back to the others. "Stay here while I scout ahead."

He crept off into the dark, while they hunkered behind a huge fallen oak.

"What if there's, like, twenty slave catchers up there?" Kristi said.

Ty let out a long breath. "Don't know."

"If we can't free Harriet, it could change the whole future, like Stephen warned."

Ty took her hand and squeezed. "We'll fix it, don't worry. We still have the time machine." He patted the time rod, which was again tied to his waist. "If we have to, we'll go back again and set things straight."

"But what if we can't? What if we just keep on making things worse—Britt and Jonah could get caught again? I won't even be *born*, then."

He squeezed her hand again. "Buck up. We'll make it right."

After thirty minutes that felt like as many hours, Kristi heard a soft rustle ahead. Bo appeared, as if out of thin air.

"It's them, alright," he said, panting. "Harriet and the others are tied to a tree."

"How many guards on them?" Ty asked.

"Three," Bo said. "And they've been celebrating. I smelled whiskey before I was even close."

"Just three." Kristi nodded. "We can take them, right? Especially if they're drunk."

Bo nodded. "One's that man Mackey. I was hoping to see him again."

"Yeah." Kristi clenched her jaw. "Me too." But Britt sank back, looking terrified.

"Don't worry." She reached for his hand. "He won't hurt you anymore."

Britt wrenched away and shook his head, mute again.

"You can stay here," Jonah said, putting a hand on his shoulder.

Britt lowered his head, but said nothing.

"What's the scheme?" Ty asked.

Bo crouched. "We circle around 'em, close in real slow. Like so." He sketched out a plan in the dirt. "When I jump, you follow. Make as much racket as you can so they think we have our own strong posse."

Leaving Britt there, they crept forward until they were a hundred yards from the fire, then split. Jonah and Bo made a wide arc to get around the other side. Kristi and Ty went straight at it.

Kristi's heart pounded so hard she was sure the slave catchers would hear. She took long, slow breaths. Clenched and unclenched her sweating palms.

The fire was huge. Its flames leapt ten feet into the night sky, spreading a circle of light fifty feet around the camp.

How are we going to get close enough? Her heart *bong*-ed harder. She slipped into the long shadow of a tree, dropped to all fours and crawled to its trunk. Still twenty feet from the camp.

Like Bo had said, Harriet, Sam, and Abigail were tied to a tree on the other side. Sam's huge frame was hunched, his back against the trunk. Abigail lay against him, cradling their child.

What will those monsters do with a baby? Kristi thought, biting her lip.

Harriet sat on Sam's other side, back straight, jaw set defiantly. The reflecting flames made her eyes look afire.

Two of the patrollers hopped around the fire, staggering, sloshing whiskey from tin cups as they danced.

"We got Moses, we got Moses!" a tall, skinny man with long, greasy hair and a shaggy beard sang out, raising his mug toward her and spilling more. "MOSES!"

"We's gonna be rich!" the other man hooted. He was shorter, stockier, with a billiard ball-shaped head and dirt-streaked face.

The two linked arms at the elbows and danced in a staggering circle.

Kristi frowned. *Where's Mackey*?

As if in answer, the man stepped into the firelight, a deep scowl furrowing his brow. "Oh, shut that racket up!"

But they kept dancing. Mackey turned toward the captives. "What're *you* lookin' at?" he growled, kicking dirt at Harriet.

Her glare didn't falter. Mackey turned away, took a long draw from his mug. His face puckered and he wiped his mouth on the back of one sleeve.

Now, Kristi thought. *Jump them now!* She eyed the skinny one. She could hit his legs and take him down just fine, just like on the soccer field.

But Mackey stepped away from the fire, right toward the tree she was hiding behind. She pressed herself into the bark, holding her breath.

Mackey stopped beside the tree and fumbled with his belt.

Eeew! She bit one finger. *Disgusting!*

But before he could get his pants down, Mackey staggered and fell against the tree. He threw both arms around the trunk—and one hand fell on Kristi's arm.

"What the—"

A deep, primal scream tore through the night. Bo appeared, running full-bore toward the two dancing men. He lowered one shoulder and rammed the taller man like a freight train, knocking him into the stout guy and taking both down. Jonah appeared an instant later and jumped onto the scrimmage pile. They rolled closer to the fire, then to the captives. Sam and Harriet stretched against their bonds and kicked dirt into the seething mass.

Kristi wrenched away from Mackey's grip and ducked around the other side of the tree. Ty ran toward Mackey, shouting, "Get away from her!"

Perhaps startled to see another white face, Mackey froze.

Kristi circled the tree and dove at the slave catcher's stomach. But Mackey recovered and stepped to one side, slamming a hand into the back of her head, driving her to the ground. Then he spun deftly, drunkenness apparently gone, and caught Ty as he lunged. Mackey flipped him over and slammed him onto his back.

Kristi pushed up to hands and knees. Her head spun from the blow. Before she could regain her feet, Mackey hauled her up and wrapped one arm around her throat. Then he dug a pistol from his belt with the other hand and fired into the air. The ear-splitting report rattled her head and she almost retched.

The four by the fire stopped fighting and stared.

"Let 'em up!" Mackey pressed the gun to the side of Kristi's head. "Let 'em up or I'll kill her!"

Bo and Jonah rolled off the other two. The short man's nose dripped blood as he staggered to his feet. He wiped it on the back of one sleeve, then turned and kicked Jonah in the stomach. The other shoved Bo back onto the ground and kicked at him, too.

"Looks like we jus' earned us another thousand dollars, boys," Mackey called. "Git some rope."

Kristi clawed at the forearm pressed to her throat, fighting to pull a breath, but the air wouldn't come. Finally, as the edges of her vision went blurry and black, he let go. She fell at his feet, gasping and coughing. He kept the gun aimed at her head.

"Don't you move," he warned Jonah and Bo.

"Kristi!" Ty scrambled over. "You okay?"

She shook her head. Hot tears gushed down her cheeks. Everything was lost.

The skinny slave catcher returned with rope. Bo and Jonah were on their knees.

"Runaways is rainin' from the sky," the short man whooped, and laughed.

"We been lookin' all over for you, boy." Mackey sneered at Jonah. "Where's yer snivelin' baby brother? Off cryin' in his—"

He never finished. A shadow burst into the light, swinging a long branch like a club. It slammed into the middle of Mackey's back with a solid *thunk*. The slave catcher howled and sprawled onto his face. The pistol skittered away.

"Yeah, Britt!" Ty hollered, jumping on Mackey's back. He grabbed a fistful of the man's long hair and slammed his face into the dirt.

Harriet kicked the back of the taller slave catcher's legs, buckling his knees. Sam shoved a foot between the legs of the other. Jonah and Bo leapt and overpowered them quickly.

Kristi knelt onto Mackey's back and pinned his arms to his sides. Britt picked up the gun. He stood shaking, breathing heavily. He looked back and forth between the gun in his hands and the slave catcher sprawled on the ground.

"You got him, Britt!" Kristi yelled. "You got him!"

Britt took a deep breath. His face hardened. He stepped forward and pressed the gun into the back of Mackey's head.

"Oh, wait—no!" Kristi cried.

Britt gripped the revolver with both hands, tears still pouring down his cheeks. "He hurt me. Beat me for no reason. He laugh when I soilt myself."

"I know," Kristi said, keeping her tone soft, even. "But that's over now. He can't hurt you anymore. And you're a better man."

Mackey squirmed and flipped over, but Kristi and Ty kept his arms pinned. The catcher looked up with wide eyes.

"He oughta die!" Britt pressed the gun to Mackey's forehead. His thumb fumbled for the hammer.

"Please!" Mackey squealed. "Please, don't! Sorry! I'm so sorry!" A giant wet spot darkened the crotch of his pants.

Kristi put a hand on top of Britt's.

"He *does* deserve it, but if you kill him, they'll never stop looking for you. You'll never be safe, no matter where you go."

"I won't hunt you no more," Mackey sobbed. "Let me go and I'll let you alone. You won't never see me again."

"Shut up!" Britt screamed.

"They'll come after Jonah, too," Kristi said. "Neither of you will ever truly be free. Tell him, Jonah!"

Britt's hand shook again. He looked toward his brother.

"You ain't no killer, Britt," Jonah said. "Don't let 'em make you one."

"But—But—"

"Gimme the gun, Britt."

"Yeah, give him the gun!" Mackey cried.

"Shut up!" Jonah kicked the slave catcher in the gut.

Britt sighed and handed the gun to Jonah.

"Thank you! Thank you! Thank you!" Mackey whimpered.

Jonah knelt and pressed the barrel of the revolver against his mouth. "Now I got the gun, *boy*. Wha'cha think o' that?"

Mackey sputtered around the barrel pressed to his lips. He wet himself again.

"Hey, looks like you soilt yerself, *massa*. Where's that whip, now?"

Mackey started blubbering.

"If I ever see your ugly face again, I ain't gonna hesitate. Hear?"

Mackey nodded vigorously and grunted, "Uh-huh."

Jonah smiled and withdrew the gun. Then he hit Mackey with the butt end, knocking him out.

* * *

They took the horses and made quick time back, riding double. By the time the bridge came into view, the sky had paled to a soft gray and birds chirped in the trees.

Fifty yards from the bank, a dozen shadows emerged from the trees and spread out in front of them.

"Halt!" commanded a deep voice.

Harriet and Jonah pulled out the guns and the men on horseback circled.

Kristi dug her nails into the saddle. *No! No! No! No! No!* She wanted to fall off the horse, kick her legs and scream. *Just leave us alone!*

"Do not fear us," the deep voice said. The man urged his horse forward and took off a round-brimmed hat, revealing stark white hair and chin whiskers. "We are *Friends.*"

Bo rode to meet him with an outstretched hand. "Hello, Mr. Garrett."

SEVENTEEN

M ake it quick," Harriet huffed. "Ain't no time for long goodbyes." With a curt nod, she pulled the blue shawl over her head, heaved up the steps of the train, and disappeared into the passenger car.

Kristi smiled around at the others. None of the history books had ever described Harriet Tubman as sentimental—or patient.

The engine's stack belched black smoke into the evening sky. Steam erupted from the sides. The whistle shrieked.

Woot –Woooooooot

"Take care of yourself, little girl," Bo said, squeezing her shoulder.

She touched the broad, capable hand. "Sure you can't go back to Thomas's farm? Mr. Garrett said he is home, now."

He shook his head. "Too many eyes'll be watchin' the old man right now. Thomas will send for me in Canada after things cool off."

She hugged his waist. "Thank you for saving them—for saving all of us. Britt and Jonah are free mainly because of you."

"Don't go thanking me yet. I got more work left before I'm done." He winked and hopped up onto the steel boarding step.

She turned to Jonah and Britt.

"So it's goodbye?" Jonah said.

Kristi threw a glance at Ty, who stood a few feet behind her. He nodded.

"I wish I could go with you all the way to St. Catharines," she said. "But—"

"Moses ain't likely to let us get lost 'long the way." Jonah smiled. Really smiled.

"You be safe now, Britt." Kristi touched the boy's arm. Then she grinned. "Don't go shooting any slave catchers."

Britt sniffed and looked down. "Thanks," he mumbled, then turned abruptly and stepped toward the train.

But Kristi wasn't letting him off so easily. She grabbed him from behind and wrapped him in the Connors' traditional bear hug. He grunted and scuffed his feet, but didn't push her off.

She finally let go. "Be safe," she whispered. He nodded and scampered onto the step, then up into the coach car.

"ALL ABOARD!"

Now only Jonah stood before her. The boy who would sire her whole family. Kristi wished she could tell him of all the things to come. About the grandson who'll fly bombers in World War II. The sons and grandsons who'll be businessmen and lawyers. And even the great-great-great granddaughter, once called White Man's Pet, who'll be a time-traveler.

She smiled at that last thought. "You watch out for Britt."

He nodded. "Sorry...for being so mean to you."

"It's okay," she winked. "Sometimes I deserved it."

Woot—Woooooooot

"Oh—you better go," she said, wanting to hug him, too, but she didn't dare.

He raised a hand. "Take care of yo'self, Pet."

She smiled. "You too."

Jonah grabbed a rail and stepped up as the train lurched and began to move away.

"You okay?" Ty said, stepping beside her.

She wiped a tear on the back of her hand. "Yeah. Fine."

"You did good," Ty said, taking her hand. "You did *real* good."

"Do you think?" she said. "But what if it still didn't work? What if history doesn't *want* Britt to be saved? I might go back and find out something else horrible happened to him, anyhow. Him *and* Jonah?"

Ty shrugged. "Then you'll just have to come back and save 'em again, won't you?"

She thought for a second, then nodded. "Yeah. I guess so."

They left the station platform, found an empty, darkened barn and went inside. Ty handed her the time rod. She pushed the round button to turn it on and the familiar blue and red lights flashed. The small screen read *12: October: 2014.*

"Guess it's time," she said.

"What're you going to do about your dad's wedding?" Ty asked.

She took a deep breath and let it out slowly. "Deal with it. It'll be fine. After this, surely I can learn to live with *Bratney*."

Ty smiled. "I'm sure you can."

"Why don't you come with me? Back to our own time, I mean." She elbowed him in the ribs. "We can be, like, time-traveling super heroes: History Girl and the Time-Warp Kid. Go wherever we want, whenever we want, and just, you know...help people."

Ty laughed. "More like *Warped Girl.*"

She hit his shoulder. "Seriously, though. Why not come back with me?"

He shook his head. "Not yet. I'm going to stay here, with Thomas. Without Bo, the old bloke's gonna need my help."

She sighed. "Yeah, I figured."

"But come back and get me before you go on any more adventures. Someone has to keep you out of trouble."

"And someone's gotta get boring old you *into* trouble every once in a while."

He smiled. "Sounds like a plan."

Kristi hugged him, then stepped back. "See you soon, Time-Warp Kid."

"Not soon enough, History Girl."

She blew a kiss, then bent the rod into a halo. The lights flashed like a solar flare. Buffeting time-winds forced her eyelids shut. She brought the halo up to her head and shot off into swirling ribbons of light.

* * *

Kristi landed with a thud on a hardwood floor, writhing and gasping as jagged fingernails seemed to scrape along the inside of her skull. After a moment, the pain abated enough for her to blink the blurring tears away. She was back in Mimi's house, curled in a ball on the floor of the empty bedroom. It was dark outside the window. The house was silent.

It was another few minutes before her aching head allowed her to sit up. The horrid powder-blue bridesmaid's dress hung on the back of the closet door. Both sleeves were attached again.

Good, she thought. *At least that's fixed.*

Wearily, she pushed to her feet and tiptoed into the hallway. If Mimi was still up, she could check the family tree, make sure Britt really *had* gotten away safely.

But her great-grandmother's door was shut, the space underneath it dark.

Guess I can wait until morning, she thought. Returning to her room, she collapsed onto the bed, the first soft thing she'd lain upon for what felt like years. She pulled up the comforter and fell into a deep sleep.

It seemed only seconds later when a hand jostled her shoulder.

"Kristi, wake up," called a voice.

"Go away," she groaned, pulling a pillow over her head.

"Come on, Kristi. Wake up." The hand jostled harder.

"*What?*" she grumbled, tossing down the pillow and opening her eyes. Standing beside the bed was a boy with short, dark hair and deep brown eyes. She flinched and sat straight up.

"Who—who are *you?*"

The boy frowned. "What?"

"Who *are* you?" she said, pulling the comforter to her chin. "What're you doing in my room?"

He laughed. "You have a bad dream or something? It's me, Britt. Your *cousin?*"

Her head spun. "B-Britt? What's going on?"

The smile fell from his face. "You feeling all right, Kristi?" He reached out to touch her forehead, but she ducked away, rolled off the other side of the bed, and hit the ground running.

"Where you going?"

She burst from the room without answering and shot down the hall. At Mimi's door, she pounded with both palms.

"Mimi! Mimi! You in there?"

A chair creaked, then came the thump of Mimi's cane. The door opened a crack. "What's all the racket, girl?"

"Please, Mimi. I—I really need to look at the family tree again."

The old woman eyed her warily, then swung the door open. "Come on in, then."

Kristi rushed past, dropped to her knees in front of the bookshelf, and dragged out the huge leather album. Hefting it with both hands, she rushed over to the bed and flopped it open across the bedspread.

"What's so important?"

"I—I can't explain yet," she said, turning the pages. She found the folded yellow paper tucked into the front pocket. Across the top of the page was *Jonah Connors*, his wife Celia, and their three children. The branches spread beneath until Kristi, her brother, and sister were listed at the bottom. Between them were all the Connors, just as they had been before. She let out a relieved breath. She hadn't messed anything up.

She picked the aged piece of paper and felt another piece folded behind. Her heart gave a jump. With another deep breath, she slowly unfolded it.

Britt Connors (1850-1904)—Chastity Connors (1845-1914)

Kristine Connors-Wilson (1868-1943)

The branches beneath Britt and his wife were heavy with descendants, dozens upon dozens of children, grandchildren, aunts, uncles, cousins—none of whom had existed, as far as she knew, before her trip to 1858. She found *Britt Samuels*, listed at the bottom, on the same level with her own name, but on the other side of the fold.

She fell back onto the bed, hugging the family tree to her chest, laughing.

THE END

EPILOGUE:
SEPTEMBER 17, 1862

The sun nudged over the far horizon, burning low-lying mist away. The valley was a green sea of rich farmland, half-grown corn, chest-high wheat, and lush green grasslands.

Sweat trickled down Ty's neck and soaked the collar of his heavy blue uniform. Going to be another scorcher. He stood behind the freshly dug earthen works, gripping the straps of his medical bag with white knuckles.

Spread across the green fields below was a mile-long line of white tents, campfires, and men in gray uniforms.

Boom

The cannon's report echoed through the valley. A tiny puff of gray smoke rose from the center of the Confederate line.

Ty turned and threw up in the dirt.

Watch out....

...for Kristi and Ty's next adventure. TIME OF WAR will be third in the American Epochs series of time-travel adventures. Coming soon from Overdue Books and Northampton House Press!

ABOUT THE AUTHOR

Todd McClimans is an elementary school principal and former fifth grade teacher. He holds bachelor's degrees in Creative Writing and Elementary Education and master's degrees in Creative Writing and Educational Leadership.

Todd lives in Pennsylvania with his wife and three kids. A self-styled history buff and fantasy nerd, he first became interested in writing about American history when teaching his fifth graders the riveting stories of patriots and their struggle for independence. He aims to bring history to life for young readers by writing stories with a careful mixture of historical fact and fantastical story-telling with characters to whom readers can relate.

Outside of his duties as principal, husband, father, and writer, Todd spends his free time (as sparse as it may be) reading, running, and riding his bike. He's an avid reader of anything fantasy and lists his current favorite authors (a list that is never exhaustive) as Lois Lowry, J.K. Rowlings, J.R.R. Tolkien, Stephen King, David McCollough, and George R.R. Martin.